Pictures of Hollis Woods

Pictures of

Hollis Woods

Patricia Reilly Giff

SCHOLASTIC INC.

New York   Toronto   London   Auckland   Sydney
Mexico City   New Delhi   Hong Kong   Buenos Aires

ISBN 0-439-57783-7

12 11 10 9 8 7 6 5 4 3 2 1   3 4 5 6 7 8/0

Printed in the U.S.A.   23

First Scholastic printing, September 2003

The text of this book is set in 14-point Fournier Monotype.
Book design by Trish Parcell Watts

For Alice Tiernan,
who fishes in the Delaware River

And for Bill Reilly,
who fishes with her

MY THANKS TO CRAIG VIRDEN,
WHOSE ADVICE, ENCOURAGEMENT, AND SUPPORT
HAVE MEANT SO MUCH TO ME,
AND ESPECIALLY FOR HIS FRIENDSHIP

First Picture

X

This picture has a dollop of peanut butter on one edge, a smear of grape jelly on the other, and an X across the whole thing. I cut it out of a magazine for homework when I was six years old. "Look for words that begin with W," my teacher, Mrs. Evans, had said.

She was the one who marked in the X, spoiling my picture. She pointed. "This is a picture of a family, Hollis. A mother, M, a father, F, a brother, B, a sister, S. They're standing in front of their house, H. I don't see one W word here."

I opened my mouth to say: How about W for wish, or W for want, or W for "Wouldn't it be loverly," like the song the music teacher had taught us?

But Mrs. Evans was at the next table by that time, shushing me over her shoulder.

"Whoo-ee!" said the kid with dirty nails who

sat next to me. "You don't know anything, Hollis Woods."

I reached for my crayon and dug an X into her picture of a snow-white washing machine. "Too bad you can't use it to get your hands clean," I said.

When I think of my W picture deep inside my backpack under all the other pictures I've drawn, I think of that poor washing machine kid who cried over her ruined picture, and the frowning Mrs. Evans, who told me to sit in the hall with a time-out T letter for the rest of that long afternoon. "You don't deserve to be with the rest of us today," she said.

I sat for a while looking at a picture of a pointy mountain. Someday I would climb a mountain like that. I'd build a little house and maybe I'd have a horse that would live right in the house with me, and a dog and a cat.

When I saw the principal coming down the hall, I picked myself up and walked out the door. The woman I was staying with—I called her the lemon lady because of the way her mouth caved in—made me stay in the yard all weekend for that. "You think you're so tough," she said. "I'll show you tough."

That foolish woman forgot that as long as I had

a pencil and paper, I'd get along. I drew her with her pursed-up lips, then tied her picture to the tree for target practice with gravel from the path.

But when I think of my W picture, mostly I think of the Regans' house in Branches. I think of the Old Man, and Izzy, and their son, Steven. All they needed to match my picture was a girl, G.

And that's what I thought the morning I ran away from them, touching the great holly bushes, feeling their sharpness, and the sticky evergreen branches that hung over the dirt road leading to town. I stopped to look up at the mountain, and then at the house half hidden in the trees, the gray porch tacked on the front, screens bellying out, the chimney leaning, the two windows upstairs that had been in my bedroom, and the river in front.

My river, the Delaware.

That day I thought I'd never see any of it again. N, never, and in my mind I drew an X over all of them, and over me, too.

CHAPTER 1

*T*he house was falling apart. I could see that from the car window. But it didn't bother me. After a while the houses ran together, four now—no, five.

There was the green house where the door didn't quite close; the wind blew in and up the stairs, rattling the window panes. The white house: crumbs on the table, kids fighting over a bag of Wonder bread. The yellow house: sooty, a long-haired woman with braids, no rugs on the stairs, the loud sound of feet going up and down.

Ah, and the house in Branches. Steven's house. But that house was different. I'd never forget that one.

Don't think about it, Steven said in my head.

I did that a lot; I pretended Steven was right there next to me when I knew he was miles away in upstate New York. I wondered if he ever said to himself, "What is Hollis Woods doing right this minute?" And did he put my words in his head?

The driver turned off the motor. For a moment we looked out at the trees, the leaves with just a tinge of red this October afternoon. "We're here, Hollis," she said, a woman in sweats, a mustard stain on the front from the hot dogs we had eaten on the side of the road. Those hot dogs were a mean lump in the middle of my stomach, sloshing around with a Mountain Dew.

She'd tried to talk all the way, but I hadn't answered. I slumped in my seat, feet up on the glove compartment, wearing an A&S baseball hat with the brim yanked low over my forehead. If someone looks into your eyes, I read in a book one time, he'll see right into your soul.

I didn't want anyone to see into my soul.

I knew she was dying to tell me to get my sneakers off her dashboard, but she didn't. She was waiting to deliver her speech.

I could hear her getting ready for it with a puff of breath. "This can be a new start, Hollis. A new place." She licked her finger and scratched at the mustard stain. "No one knows you. You can be different, you can be good, know what I mean?"

Maybe she gave that speech to every foster kid in every driveway as she dumped them off like the UPS guy dumping off packages on a busy day, but I didn't think so. I had looked into her eyes once, just the quickest look, and I had seen that she felt sorry for me, that she didn't know what to do with me. Too bad for you, mustard woman.

I hummed a little of "The Worms Crawl In, the Worms Crawl Out."

"She was an art teacher," the mustard woman said, pointing to the house. "Retired now. I've never met her, but everyone at the agency says she's wonderful with kids . . ." Her voice trailed off, but I knew she had meant to say "kids like you."

I walked my feet up the dashboard so my knees came close to my chin.

"No one's been here with her for a while, but Emmy said it would be a good place for you."

Emmy, the agency hotshot. She had probably said, "What have we got to lose?"

"A good place for an artist like you, Hollis," the mustard woman said. "Mr. Regan . . ."

I drew in my breath. The Old Man. I closed my eyes as if I were ready to doze off.

"He wanted you to have a chance to work at your drawings. He said it would be a crime if you didn't."

I tried to yawn, but then the front door opened, and a woman came out on the porch with a mangy orange cat one step behind her. I didn't bother to give them more than a glance. What did I care what the woman looked like?

But next to me, the mustard woman took a deep breath. I cut my eyes in the direction of the house. I was good at that, seeing everything without turning my head, without looking up, without blinking.

I did blink then, of course I did. Anyone getting a first look at Josie Cahill would do the same. It wasn't just that she was movie-star beautiful, or that she was wearing a blue dress made of filmy stuff that floated around her, and rings on eight of her fingers. It was this: She had a knife in one hand. She held it in front of her so it caught the glint of late-afternoon sunshine and became a silvery light itself.

"Lordy," the mustard woman breathed.

I sat up straight, wondering if I should open the car door and run, or reach out to push the button down, locking myself in.

The knife woman came close enough for me to see that the movie-star face had dozens of tiny crisscross lines on its cheeks and across its forehead.

But then she smiled, and the lines around her mouth rearranged themselves. She leaned forward and put one hand on the car window. "Hollis," she said. "Are you here, then?"

I couldn't take my eyes off her. I could feel a pencil in my hand, moving across the paper, drawing her face, her eyes, the knife. I reached over the seat, grabbed my backpack, and was out the door, slamming it behind me.

On the other side of the car the mustard woman was out too.

"Tea?" the movie star asked the mustard woman as if she were reading her grocery list. "Coffee? Lemonade? Orange juice?"

The mustard woman shook her head. She was still thinking about the knife. "I just want to get Hollis settled," she said uneasily.

"I'm settled," I said.

We all stood there for another few minutes, the mustard woman trying to fill the space around us with talk. Then at last she opened the car door again and was gone.

"Want to call me Josie?" The movie star rubbed her forehead absently with the knife handle. "If you want to do the Cahill part you say it 'Kale,' you know, like that vegetable." She jerked her head toward the cat. "That's Henry. He's a little irritable sometimes."

I followed her up the path and around to the back of the house. Henry came too, reaching out to stab my leg with one irritable claw.

Josie looked back over her shoulder. "Hungry?"

I shook my head; the hot dogs were just settling in.

"Drop your things," she said, waving the knife. "We'll get them later."

In back of the house was a different world: a garden on the edge of the woods, woods so small I could see around them to houses on the next street.

"I've lived here"—Josie raised one eyebrow—"since they invented the spoon."

"Who did that, anyway?" I asked, trying her out.

Her other eyebrow shot up. "The knife and fork people, who else?"

I could feel a laugh coming as she waved her hand. "This is my place."

Carved tree branches were stuck in the dirt in front of the woods, some of them thicker than my arm, others almost pencil-thin. All of them had faces, and bits of grass or wreaths of flowers circled their wooden heads.

I touched this one and that, using two fingers, the ones I used to shadow in my own drawings. One of the figures had a filmy scarf around its neck and held a bird's nest in its bent arms. "You?" I asked.

She patted the scarf and turned to look at me, head tilted.

I pulled my hat down over my eyes and stared at her figures. She really was an artist.

"I'll make one of you," Josie Cahill said. "We'll have to find the right piece of wood. I think there's one in the back. The shape of the head is there already, the nose sharp, and the eyes . . ." She stopped. "But only if you stay. It will take weeks for me to do. Months, maybe."

I tried to think of what to say. I never stayed anywhere for long before I ran. One morning I'd wake up and I'd have had enough. I'd grab my backpack and go. I'd hang out in the city, see a couple of movies, or if the weather was nice, I'd head over to Jones Beach and sleep under the boardwalk. Sometimes it took them days to find me. But they never sent me back to the same place. The people in their houses had probably had enough of me, too.

Josie waited for me to answer.

I raised one shoulder. "I'm not sure."

"Henry and I will treat you like our best company for as long as you stay," she said.

Henry crouched at the top of the path, eyes slitted, tail switching at me. "I'm glad he's not a tiger," I said, feeling that laughter again.

Josie's eyes danced. "Maybe we'll go back and cut that piece of wood anyway."

A table leaned against the back of the house, an old

redwood table with tools: a drill, an ax, and knives sharp enough to split hairs.

I reached for the ax, then followed Josie Cahill into the woods.

And in my head I told Steven, *I may just stay for a while. What do you think of that?*

Second Picture

Steven

This wasn't one picture, it was six, eight, ten. I never could get Steven right. I could see him in my head, though, close my eyes and there he was.

That first day, I was sick to my stomach from the smell of the bus, the dizzying mountain roads. I had been on that bus for hours. It seemed like weeks. The tag pinned to my shirt, HOLLIS WOODS, LONG ISLAND, had rubbed a raw patch into my neck.

All I could think about was how thirsty I felt. I imagined ice cubes in my mouth, burning my tongue, ginger ale in a glass that was wet to the touch, root beer with two scoops of orange sherbet.

I was on my way to a place called Branches to spend the summer with a family named Regan.

"I'll be good if you don't make me go," I had almost told the woman I was living with in the

stucco house. "I won't make a sound, you'll see."
Instead, I squeezed my lips in between my teeth so
hard they were hidden inside my mouth, and shot
lightning rays at her out of the corners of my eyes.

"Fresh air, a place in the country," the stucco
woman said, "that's what you need."

She didn't mean it, though. I heard her on the
phone. "Two months," she said, "two months to
do what I please and not have to worry about that
kid getting into everyting."

"Everything," I said, putting my tongue
against my top teeth in front of her face.

"Fresh." She cupped her hand over the phone.
"Fresh as paint."

And back to the phone, whispering now: "No
wonder she hasn't been adopted. She's a mountain
of trouble, that Hollis Woods."

I marched up the stairs, hitting every rung with
her lime green umbrella.

Anyway, I was the last one left on the bus. Up
in front the driver talked with the woman from the
agency. If I ducked down in back of the seat,
would they forget about me? Would they turn
around and go back to Long Island?

We lumbered up the main street of Hancock,
passing a row of houses and a movie theater, and

came to a stop in front of a diner. "Straighten up, kid," the bus driver said, looking into the rear-view mirror. "We're here."

I gathered up my backpack and the plastic bag they had given me: a toothbrush, a bar of soap that smelled like an old sock, a pink washcloth, and a book for drooling two-year-olds, Kelly Goes to Camp. I tossed the book in the agency woman's lap as I passed, nose in the air, pretending I wasn't dying of thirst, pretending I wasn't bursting from having to go to the bathroom.

Outside the bus window a man leaned against the wall of the diner, his hat over his eyes, and a boy played handball against a brick wall. I climbed down into the blistering hot sun, checking out the boy. A skinny mess he was, much taller than I, his socks falling down. They looked as if they didn't even match.

As the bus started up, the exhaust smelling like a sewer, the boy slammed the ball against the wall, missing it on its way back. He nearly killed himself trying to dive in front of the bus for it, then jumped back at the last moment as the ball bounced across the street.

I put down my backpack and the agency freebie bag, darted across the street in back of the bus, and scooped up the ball with one hand. I trotted back to *them, tossing it over my head and catching it a couple of times just to show them what I could do.*

The man pushed his hat back and grinned at me. He had a great face to draw: eyes the color of cinnamon toast, a prickly gray-black beard, deep laugh lines.

"I'm Steven Regan," the boy said, grinning. "How'd you get a name like that, Hollis Woods, crazy name? Do they call you Holly? We have a pile of holly bushes out in front. Touch the leaves and they draw blood. I'm going to call you Holly."

The man shook his head. "Steven."

"Try it," I cut in.

"How old are you anyway?" Steven asked, his eyes caramel behind his glasses. "You look like kind of a shrimp to me."

"Twelve," I said, bumping it up almost a year, "and tough."

"Baby. I'll be thirteen December twenty-sixth." He rushed on. "We're having lunch at the diner. My mother stayed in Branches."

"Izzy's making carrot cake," the man said.

I thought about saying I hated carrots—not true, I ate anything. Anyting, *the stucco house lady would say. Besides, they were standing there, Steven and his father, looking so pleased about having lunch in the diner and carrot cake for* dinner, I didn't have the heart, and I really had to go to the bathroom.

"Bet you're thirsty." Steven's eyes narrowed. "They've got checkers at every table. I'll play you, beat you."

He wanted to pay me back for the ball trick.

His father frowned. He knew it too.

But I was all right with it; I was fine with it.

I skittered into the diner, straight to the rest room, and then sat with them at their table drinking root beer floats, cold and sweet, with wet napkins underneath the glasses. After I had downed half of mine, Steven ticked off the things he wanted me to know. "I call the old man Pop," he said.

"You can call me that," the father said.

I took a chance. "I'm going to call you Old Man."

He laughed. "Try it." I could tell he didn't mind, though.

"What's next is I'm a walker," Steven said. "Walk myself all over Branches. I'll walk you, too."

"Maybe," I said.

"I know motors," he said. "I drive a truck."

"Don't believe that." The Old Man snorted. "Not even thirteen years old."

"I almost drive, then," Steven said, giving me a wink. "Legal any day now."

The Old Man rolled his eyes at me.

"And the last thing, I know tracks." Steven spread his arms wide. "Animal tracks. All of them."

I was laughing. I knew he meant for me to laugh. He pushed the black checkers over to me. "Let's see what you can do here, Hollis Woods," he said. "Win and I'll teach you how to drive."

"In your dreams," the Old Man said.

We played a couple of checkers games, Steven taking wild chances, while we dripped ketchup from our hamburgers onto the table and the Old Man egged us on.

Anyway, the picture I was trying for was Steven playing checkers with me that first day. That was the picture I could never get perfect. Maybe it was because he let me win that first game; maybe it was because I let him win the next one. And maybe it was because for the first time I really saw what it might be like to have a brother.

The Time with Josie

CHAPTER 2

I had been at Josie Cahill's house for three weeks. One morning when I awoke, I realized my thumb was blistered, but I didn't mind. We'd been cleaning up the grove of trees. I liked the feeling of hacking and slashing and getting things done. A pile of wood rested under Josie's back table now. "Not all of it is for whittling," she had told me. "As soon as it's really cold, we'll make enormous fires in the fireplace."

I knew she was wondering if I'd still be there when the cold came.

I wondered too.

I stretched, not ready to get up, and looked around the bedroom. It was wonderful, the first place the sun hit every day, so that squares of light turned the room to lemon gold. I stayed under the rose-and-white quilt for a few moments, then pulled on my clothes to go down to the kitchen.

Josie was bent over the table, eyeglasses perched on the end of her nose, working on a piece of wood. From the hall I could see her reflection in the kitchen window. She knew I was there but she just cut another sliver off the wood and blew it away.

I slid onto a seat opposite her at the table. In front of me were a box of cereal, two bananas, and a Danish neatly cut in half. The Danish was a little stale and the bananas beginning to freckle. Other days chocolate chips were sprinkled into the cereal, but they must have been all gone.

Still, it was a terrific breakfast, with Rice Krispies crackling in the speckled bowl. Fall leaves swept across the garden, and Josie's plane went across the wood with a *swish-swish* sound.

I sat there with my mouth full, looking around at her kitchen. It was like the rest of the house, filled with surprises: The walls were creamy yellow, and ships sailed along blue ocean moldings. A painted pelican was perched over the stove.

The pelican looked as irritable as Henry.

I told myself I'd have a house like that one day: hatboxes and wigs drawn on one bathroom wall, and high-heeled shoes, dozens of them, marching along in watercolor in a tiny bedroom at the end of the hall.

That yellow kitchen was huge. A couch sat under the window, piled high with embroidered pillows that said things like HENRY'S HOME, V FOR VICTORY, SAVE THE SARGASSO SEA.

I'd never even heard of the Sargasso Sea.

I had drawn the house with paper from my backpack and fat bits of charcoal I had found somewhere. It was lovely to sketch the house, and Josie with her scarf. She watched me sometimes as I drew Henry sitting on top of the old-fashioned radio, and the pelican with beady eyes.

Too bad you don't have your drawing box, I imagined Steven saying, *all those yellows and blues.*

I was all right, though.

"We'll take a drive in the Silver Bullet today," Josie said, sounding pleased with herself. She brushed a few shavings off the front of her dress onto the faded linoleum floor. "I have things to show you, Hollis."

No school on a Monday? I shrugged to myself. If she wanted to forget about it, that was fine with me. I spent most of the time in the back of the classroom sketching, or drawing faces in ink on the plastic desk and erasing them with one wet finger.

I had taken only two days off so far, reminding myself that the mustard woman would probably be checking up on me. And the absence notes I wrote myself and signed in a spidery hand that looked like Josie's were masterpieces: *Hollis had a high fever over the weekend. Please send her home if she looks flushed.* Or *Hollis had a severe rash. We learned that she's allergic to tomatoes. Pity. She really enjoys them.*

I shoved the last of a banana into my mouth and watched as Josie plopped a straw hat with a rose onto her head and wrapped one of those filmy scarves twice around her neck; then I followed her out to the garage.

The car was ancient, a Buick from the eighties. The fenders were dented and a streak of white paint ran across the door, but inside, the seats were soft and furry, and hanging from the windshield was a small tree figure of a man with gray whiskers. No, not a man. It was Henry standing on his back legs.

"I put acorn boxing gloves on him but they kept falling off," Josie said. "You don't have to worry about Henry. Henry's ready to stick up for you whenever the chips are down."

I had to laugh, thinking about Henry in boxing gloves fighting for me. My main concern about Henry was how to keep out of his way. I stepped back as he jumped into the car and hopped across the backseat to sit on the rear window ledge, his head up, one notched ear forward, his whiskers twitching.

But I didn't have time to think about that. I slid into

the car as Josie backed out of the garage and down the driveway in one great swoop and, never looking, barreled onto the street.

You wouldn't believe this, I told Steven in my head, and grabbed the edge of my seat with both hands.

Josie began to talk, glancing down at her movie-star hands, long and thin, her nails painted fire-engine red but chipping here and there. I wanted to tell her to slow down but bit my lip instead.

I thought I was going to be dead by the time we reached the first crossing. But by the second corner I realized there wasn't that much traffic, and the few cars on the road stayed well out of our way, so I began to relax and listen to what she was saying.

"Going to stay and have yourself done up in a tree?" she asked. "Stay longer and I'll teach you how to drive. Like the movies? We can do that, too."

My mouth went dry. *How to drive?* That's what Steven would say. *You could tell her a story about that, couldn't you?*

I brushed at the air, wanting to brush him out of my head. I was trying to think of what illness I'd give myself today, when the Silver Bullet turned another corner and stopped. Spread out in front of us was a canal with a few fishing boats, kerosene trails sliding out in back of them on the water, and beyond the boats, beyond the canal, was more water than I had ever seen.

It moved and rolled, it shimmered, it glowed iridescent silver. The Atlantic Ocean. I itched for a piece of
drawing paper.

"This is my ocean," Josie said, as if it belonged to
her personally, like one of her hats.

It was the way I felt about the Delaware River. A
pain filled my chest as I thought about it. I wanted to
sit in the Old Man's rowboat, to lean over and put my
hands into that clear water, to watch the catfish riding
along on the bottom, the schools of pickerel lazing in
the warm sun.

"So what do you think?" Josie asked.

"Bigger than a river," I said. "Rougher." I spread
out my hands, trying to think of the difference. "It's
wonderful, but . . ."

She waited.

"You can't get your arms around it."

"Ah," she said, stopping to think. "There are salt-
water people, and freshwater people." She held up her
hand. "Then there are some who don't even know
enough to fall in love with the water." She looked at
me with satisfaction. "But they're not us."

I nodded, thinking of how the river might look as it
reflected the last of the fall leaves.

"We'll get out," Josie said, "and walk along the
jetty." She was singing under her breath now, a bit of a
song I had learned somewhere. "By the sea, by the sea."

Henry followed us as we went toward the jetty, a path to the sea made of huge boulders tumbled one on top of the other. They were slippery, those rocks, with places your feet could get caught, and I wondered if I should help Josie climb up. But she didn't need help. She swung herself up next to me, her scarf blowing in the wind coming off the sea. "Just breathe," she said.

She didn't have to tell me. I had never smelled anything like that air: fish, and kerosene, and salt.

"I don't know what I'd do without the ocean," she said.

And then we skittered out to where I couldn't see anything but water in front of us. Josie pointed down with one foot. Between the rocks were pockets of water, and some of them had tiny fish swimming around in them, fish so small they were blurs of pewter. In one pool was a crab whose claws were no bigger than my pinky nails.

I knelt down on the edge of a boulder and put my fingers into the water, watching their reflection as the water moved, feeling the spray on my shirt. Was there snow on the mountain yet?

Don't think about the mountain.

I thought about Steven and the Old Man and Izzy and I put my hand on my chest because there was such an ache inside.

Josie was a statue standing above me, holding her hat against the wind, her eyes closed, a half smile on her face.

"I thought maybe I'd stay for a while," I said slowly. "As long as you want me to, that is."

Josie opened her eyes and beamed down at me.

"So if you'd like to work on my tree figure . . ."

She raised her hand to her scarf. "I've already started."

And I knew Steven would be saying, *What are you doing, Hollis?*

Third Picture

Fishing in the Delaware River

The river meandered along in front of the Regans' summer house, and on the opposite side was the Old Man's mountain.

What was it about that mountain? Coming from Long Island, I had never gotten within yelling distance of anything more than a hill. So why did this mountain look so familiar? I stretched my neck to look up and up at its rocky self mostly covered with evergreens.

"You'll fall over," Steven said.

I shrugged, reaching for my backpack. Inside were a bunch of colored pencils, stubby things I had collected wherever I could find them. It would take six of them, blues and greens and grays, to get the color of the river the way it was the first time I saw it.

"Do you know how to fish?" Steven asked.

"If I wanted to." I squinted at the river; didn't

know how to fish, didn't know how to swim. I was still trying to figure out how to stay away from that water when the Old Man brought the fishing rods out of the shed.

Izzy Regan, the mother, came out onto the porch, the screen door slamming behind her. She waved at us. "Hey, guys, catch me something to go with pole beans and corn on the cob."

"Yuck to the beans," Steven said.

"I like pole beans," I said. I'd heard of pole-cats, but never pole beans.

Izzy nodded at me. "It's great to have a girl around, Holly. We have to stick together against these guys."

Izzy was the tallest woman I'd ever seen. Her blond hair was wrapped around her head, and she seemed to be smiling just for me.

And then we were down on the bank, barefoot, standing in the shade of a few scrub pines. The Old Man put a rod threaded with a lure into my hand. "The best one," he said. "This is for luck."

He showed me how to cast so my arm went back and over my head and the line sang out. I watched the feathery lure glide on the water, and then did it again, and again.

I could see the bottom of the river. I could stand on that soft sand dotted with rocks, I thought, and be safe. I put one foot into the cool water and then the other, feeling tiny fish nibbling at my ankles. Across the way was the mountain, tall and green.

"Pop's mountain," Steven said. "I'll show you tomorrow. There's a road going up . . ."

The Old Man tightened his mouth. "Be careful of that road. I'm afraid of it."

Steven twitched one shoulder. "I'm not afraid of anything."

Anyting, I thought. The stucco house woman seemed a world away.

We stood there, the Old Man pointing to a catfish nosing its way along, then a frog sunning itself on a rock, and I closed my eyes. I knew the East Branch of the Delaware River was home.

Like a miracle I caught my first fish that afternoon. Hooked it and watched the silver curve as it broke the surface of the water. It was a huge fish, and Steven said, "Bet you a buck you can't hold on to it."

He was right there with the net, though, wanting me to get it, as I slipped on the rocks, feeling the water on my legs and then my back as I slid. I tried to get my balance with one hand, my feet going out from under me, not sure how deep the river was, wondering if my head would go under.

Steven's arm was on my elbow then, holding

me up, and the Old Man called, "You're all right, Hollis."

My feet anchored into the sand then. I edged myself back, pulling on the rod, and then the fish was mine.

Steven poured a pailful of cool water over my head so my hair was dripping, my clothes soaked. The Old Man was smiling, nodding, and Izzy came down to the bank to see what was going on.

Later I drew it all, and whenever I look at the picture I remember the taste of the fish that night, grilled on the coals, my feet bare under the porch table, and in front of us, the river. I remember Izzy touching my shoulder as she stood up to get something from the kitchen.

Why did I have to mess everything up?

The Time with Josie

*E*very night we ate soup from a can, Josie, Henry, and I. We sat at the table under a stained-glass lamp that tossed rainbows onto the kitchen ceiling. On the wall was a quick picture of Henry I had drawn. He was wearing boxing gloves and batting at the light cord.

Josie whittled away on a slice of wood as we dunked bits of donuts or slice-and-bake chocolate chip cookies into the tomato soup. On Josie's check days we ate big.

"We shouldn't do this," I told her as we trundled home a cartload of donuts, a case of cat food, and our check-day treat: a gallon of cherry vanilla ice cream and enough Snickers bars to keep us chewing for a week of television nights. "We should spread it out."

Josie didn't answer. She hummed a scrap of an old song I had never heard before. That's the way she talked sometimes. She'd start with bits of this and that, it could even be poetry. You had to untangle her words in your head like balls of knotted string. And sometimes she'd break off in the middle of a sentence, small frown lines on her forehead.

I knew something the mustard woman didn't know, something even Emmy, star of the agency, hadn't guessed. Josie forgot things, forgot words, forgot what she was doing. Not all the time, but still too often. Josie knew it too. She'd look at me helplessly, hands in the air, and then I'd rush to finish her sentence for her or to turn down the flame under a pot of soup that was ready to boil over.

"My cousin Beatrice is waiting," she sang one night, and handed me my jacket. She gave her straw hat a twirl as she passed the hook it hung on in the hall. "Much too cold for this."

"Where are we going?" I asked.

"To the movies."

"What will we use for money?"

Josie didn't answer. She pulled a brown hat out of the closet and stood at the mirror, arranging the veil in front of her eyes. In the dim light of the hall, she looked young; her skin seemed to glow.

She saw me staring at her, and for the barest second before I looked away, I could see that her eyes gleamed. "Wait a minute." She reached out and gently took my arm so I stood in front of the mirror.

I didn't much like to look at myself; there was that scar just healed from the accident on the Old Man's mountain. If I didn't see the scar, I didn't have to think about that night and the terrible sound of the truck slamming into the rocks as we slid toward the edge.

Josie took the brown hat off her head and put it on mine. She fluffed out the veil so it covered my face down to my nose and then she stood back.

I drew in my breath at the reflection. No scar, no freckles, and my sandy hair, which usually poked out in all directions, looked soft, almost curly. I looked different, almost . . . *Pretty* wasn't even the word.

"Ah," Josie said. "You know it too. This is the way you're going to look very soon. This is the way you'll look for the rest of your life. You have a beautiful face."

I swallowed. I didn't want to take the hat off. I wanted to leave it on forever.

"Wear it." She patted my shoulder, then opened the closet door to take out another hat for herself, a green wool one with flecks of gold and an iridescent clip on one side. She smiled at me. "It's yours to have forever, even when you leave me."

"I won't leave," I said.

She started to say something, but instead fiddled with the lock on the front door and dropped the key into her pocketbook. As we went past the garage, she shook her head regretfully. The gas gauge was almost on Empty—I had seen that the other day—and we had about forty cents to last us until the middle of the month.

I sighed. I had money Josie didn't know about. I always had money; I called it my running money. It couldn't be used for gas or food, just running. I had made that bargain with myself a long time ago.

We rushed along in the misty rain for a couple of blocks; then Josie stepped into the middle of the street, her head up, her hands out. "Look."

I put my head back to see a fine sleet dropping from the dark sky, streaks of white light.

How would I draw that? I wondered. Black paper, if I could get my hands on some, maybe with white tempera, or maybe the palest gray with a sable brush.

Behind us a horn blared, a loud, frightening sound. Josie grabbed my hand and we darted out of the street. Strange to feel someone's hand holding mine. The last time was Izzy's. *"I always wanted a daughter,"* she had said, hands out. *"Babies, children. Piles of them."*

Josie and I made right turns at the next three corners. Then in front of us was the Island Theater, with small lights, blurred in the mist, that ran around the marquee.

An old woman sat at the ticket counter. Not as old as Josie, but still her hair was a bundle of braided cotton candy on top of her head, and when she smiled her teeth were butter yellow. Her thumb pointed at me. "What's her name, Josie?"

"Hollis." Josie waved her hand at the woman. "This is Beatrice Gilcrest, my couin and best lifetime friend, not counting Henry."

"Gorgeous," Beatrice told Josie, and it took me a moment to realize she meant me. She leaned forward. "I would have seen you sooner, much sooner, but I've had a miserable cold." She winked at me. "I didn't want to spread my germs around."

We smiled at each other; then without paying Josie and I tiptoed past her and went inside.

I peered at the dark theater that stretched out in front of us. Almost no one else was there. It was a school night, and everyone was home, I guessed, still having supper, still doing homework. It gave me a strange feeling. I thought about Steven at the dinner table with Izzy and the Old Man, or bent over a sheet of paper working on algebra.

"We have to work to pay our way," Josie said, leading me to the candy counter. She turned on the lights, poured a pile of corn and a cup of what looked like parsley into the popcorn machine, then sat back on a high stool behind the counter. "Special recipe, this popcorn." She nodded. "Beatrice and I dreamed it up last winter."

Josie pointed up. "Beatrice lives upstairs. Her apartment takes up the whole top. It's like a bowling alley." She shook her head. "Can you imagine?"

I nodded, reaching for a kernel of popcorn. It tasted better than it looked.

A few minutes later, six or seven people came in. Josie poured popcorn into wrinkled paper bags for them, her mouth full, and then music blared and the movie came on.

Afterward we walked home, watching the mist swirl around the bare branches above us. "That was a tearjerker," Josie said.

I nodded, thinking about it: the story of a boy and a dog and Christmas in a small town in New Jersey.

"Henry would feel terrible if we brought a dog into the house," Josie said, gliding around the icy puddles next to me.

"I know." I was getting used to Henry. He spent almost every night on my bed now, and as long as I didn't stretch out my feet he didn't attack.

"But we can have Christmas," Josie said. "I have ornaments in the attic, and an artificial tree. You've never seen the attic. What treasures." She stopped, her face up to bathe in the sleet so it coated her eyelashes. "There's one ornament, a Santa Claus, Beatrice and I put it on the tree first every year." She twirled around, arms up, dipping her graceful hands.

I had that strange feeling again. Everyone was home doing homework for school tomorrow, and I was watching an old lady dance in the street.

I comforted myself with the thought of sitting in Josie's living room after supper every night, sweet chocolate melting on our tongues, wood shavings around our feet.

It's enough, I told Steven in my head, *more than enough*. I tried not to think of my *W* picture with the mother, the father, the brother, and the sister.

Fourth Picture

The Old Man's Mountain

I sat on the porch steps drawing the mountain while I waited for Steven. He was hanging over the motor of the Old Man's truck, fiddling with hoses or connections, muttering to himself. "If he'd let me drive this thing for half a minute, I'd know exactly what's wrong with it."

Half the arguments in that house had to do with Steven's wanting to drive the truck. "Right here on the property, that's all," he'd say. "No big deal." The other arguments had to do with his disappearing. It made the Old Man crazy. Up on the mountain road to follow a deer path, lying on the bottom of the rowboat to drift along searching for the kingfisher, gone somewhere and dragging me along with him.

One night at dinner the Old Man had dropped the box in my lap: tan leather, with dozens of pencils inside, points sharp and perfect, in every color you could imagine, a thick pad of paper, erasers, a pencil sharpener. I had picked up one of the pencils: French Blue, a soft color that was almost purple. "I love this," I told him.

I had wanted to throw my arms around him, wanted to tell him I had never had a present like this before, no one had. I wanted to tell him but didn't tell him; I ducked my head, my bangs a fringe over my eyes. But he knew; I knew he knew.

The Old Man was an artist, but a different kind. He drew circles and lines and squares that turned into plans for houses and buildings. He said he wished he could do what I did.

Now Steven flew around the side of the truck like one of Izzy's hens, his eyeglasses taped to the side of his head, his hands filthy from the truck. "Move it, Hollis Woods," he said. "We don't have all day here, you know."

I put the mountain picture carefully inside the box. At the end of the summer I'd give it to the Old Man as a present.

Don't think about the end of the summer, I told myself.

Steven and I raced each other down the road, across the bridge, dead tie, and stopped, out of breath, at the mountain road. After a moment we started up.

Steven lurched along. At one turn in the road he was all speed; the next he'd stop short, bent over, nose almost touching the ground. "Look at this, Holly, it's a raccoon print," he'd say, or, "See the way this branch is cut off? Beaver, building a den where the stream comes off the mountain."

The Old Man was right about the road: It was slippery, muddy in the shade, one side ready to slide off the mountain straight into the river. But worth it. "We going all the way to the top?" I drew in my breath. Did I want to do that, stand on top of the mountain, a mountain of trouble myself?

Steven shook his head. "Pop would have a fit." He ran his hand over an imaginary beard. "The rocks fall, Steven, use your head," he said in the Old Man's voice.

Halfway up was a spot that widened. We looked down and saw the house, and Izzy picking tomatoes, and we whistled at her until she waved, even though she couldn't see us.

Then we sank down on a rock and Steven fished in his pocket for a squished Hershey bar. "Should I give you half?" he asked. "You're not as big as I am."

"Give me all," I told him, laughing. "I'm more deserving."

He held up both pieces, squinting. "The Old Man would say that."

I knew that. Somehow the Old Man thought I was a great kid. How had that happened? I swallowed, thinking of the lemon lady: "You want tough?" *she had said.* "I'll show you tough."
And someone else, I didn't even remember who it was: "You've missed school half the term, how do you think you can get away with all this?"

But I was a new person with the Old Man, with Izzy, with Steven. It was as if the angry Hollis were seeping right out of my bones, leaving chocolate as soft as that sticky Hershey bar.

I looked at Steven, wondering if he minded that the Old Man thought I was great. But Steven was splitting the candy bar, and he gave me the bigger piece but did it quickly. I wasn't supposed to know. I took a breath.

I thought about the W picture in my backpack: the mother, the father, the brother, the sister.

And don't think of that, either, I told myself.

The Time with Josie

CHAPTER 4

"Company's coming," Josie said.

I looked up from my pad. I was drawing a picture of a boat I had seen at Josie's canal: white with thin blue lines of trim, the name in script on back, *Danbar-J*, and the captain hosing down the deck. I couldn't remember what he actually looked like, so I sketched in his back, bent over, a watch cap on his head.

"Who's coming?" I asked, but Josie had pattered away down the hall, with Henry following her.

"It's Monday, right?" she called back.

"It is," I said, squiggling the pencil for shadow.

"The movie is closed. My cousin Beatrice comes on Mondays." She smiled. "I forgot. You don't know that. Remember, Beatrice had a lingering cold?"

Ah, I thought. A lingering cold. Perfect for my next absence note. I looked around the kitchen. "Not much to eat in here."

She came back into the kitchen, a thin line of red on her lips. "Ah, but Beatrice brings dinner. Wait and see. It will be . . ." She patted her lips together.

"Delicious?"

She frowned. "Yes, but . . ."

"Ah," I said, trying to guess. "Stew? Pasta? Hero sandwiches?"

She shook her head. "Delicious."

I finished my drawing and propped it up on the counter to see what I thought about it. And then I heard the back door, Beatrice bustling in, her arms laden with bags, and the smell . . .

"Chinese food," I told Josie.

"Of course," she said. "That's what we always have."

I put the plates out, the knives and forks, and Josie ladled the food into bowls: cashew chicken, moo goo gai pan, bean curd, the smells making my mouth water.

Beatrice stood in back of me. I looked over my shoulder. She was leaning over, her head tilted, looking at my picture. "Did you draw this?"

I nodded.

She took off her glasses and chewed on one stem. "Surprising, isn't it?" she asked Josie.

"More than that," Josie said, beaming, moving Henry off her chair before she sat down.

As I reached for a shrimp roll, Beatrice slid into the seat opposite me and spooned rice onto my plate, the picture still in her hand.

"Don't eat," she said.

I raised my eyebrows.

"Not yet. Trot out some more of your pictures, please."

I went into Josie's peach living room with the lilac couch. We had tacked up a few of the pictures I'd done: Henry and the pelican, the rock jetties, Josie's thin tree figures in the back garden.

I pulled out the tacks and brought the drawings into the kitchen. There was no room for them on the table, so I pulled up an extra chair and piled them on that.

"Now you can eat," Beatrice said, reaching for the top one.

"Thank you." I scooped up the chicken, piling as many cashews as I could on the spoon.

She didn't eat, not until she had looked at all of them, holding each one up to the light. Josie kept nodding, reaching over with her fork to point at a line or a figure.

And then Beatrice sat back. "Imagine. I never saw anyone who was able to do this," she said, "and I was an art teacher for forty years."

"We taught that long?" Josie said.

"Forty-four for you." Beatrice brushed at her hair. "But did I ever once . . ."

"No, neither did I." Josie smiled at me, reaching across to touch my wrist with one hand.

Beatrice took a forkful of food, eating absently, staring at me the whole time. "We worked with all those kids who didn't have any concept of perspective, or even if they had that, the composition was all wrong. If only you'd been in one of those classes, Hollis." She shook her head, then smiled at Josie. "Never mind, she's here's now."

I couldn't swallow what was in my mouth. It was there in a lump, almost as large as the lump in my throat. "Thank you," I managed to say.

They were both looking at me, at the tears in my eyes.

"Spicy, that chicken," Beatrice said.

I managed to nod, to chew, at last to swallow, thinking of the Old Man: *"Where'd you ever learn to do that?"* And Izzie. *"You have a gift, pure and simple."*

After dinner Beatrice spread the pictures out on the table, reaching for my pad on the counter, one eyebrow raised to ask if she could have a piece of paper. With a twist of her pencil she showed me how to deepen the shadows on a drawing of the sea.

"Do it on my drawing," I said.

"Never," she told me. "It's your world, it belongs to you." She ran the pencil through her hair, separating the thick strands. "Drawing is what you see of the world, truly see."

"Yes, maybe," I said, not sure what she meant.

"And sometimes what you see is so deep in your head you're not even sure of what you're seeing. But when it's down there on paper, and you look at it, really look, you'll see the way things are."

I frowned. "Look at a picture one way and you'll see one thing," I said. "Look again and you might see something else. That's what the Old Man . . ." I shook my head. "A friend of mine said that once."

"Ah, yes," Beatrice said, sketching in an eye, bushy eyebrows, sharp lashes as she spoke. "But that's the world, isn't it? You have to keep looking to find the truth." She ran one pinky finger over the eyebrow; the pencil smeared just enough to curve it upward, almost like a question mark; the other pinky softened the lashes.

I watched her, fascinated. "And something else," she said. "You, the artist, can't hide from the world, because you're putting yourself down there too."

"I'm not hiding," I said, my eyes sliding away from her.

She laughed. "Good thing, because your soul is right there in front of you." She pointed to the sketch

I'd drawn of Josie in her scarf. "You see, it's what you think of her." She turned to Josie. "Maybe I can take that trip now, leave you in Hollis's hands. She loves you already."

I could see that Josie didn't know what Beatrice meant. "A trip?"

"To the Southwest."

Josie nodded then. "Yes. Adobe houses, desert, flat rocks everywhere."

"I'll paint them all," Beatrice said.

I looked from one to the other. Beatrice had picked up the pencil again, sketching herself, drawing a suitcase in her hand. And then she looked at me once more. "You're going to be something, you and that language you speak on paper." She drew her other hand waving. "I love what you have to say, Hollis Woods."

I sat there, hardly breathing.

"You have that," she said. "It's more than most people ever have. Count yourself lucky."

Fifth Picture

The Old Man

I thought I was alone, sitting on the bottom step in front of the house, drawing the Old Man, working with a flesh-peach pencil. Quick sketches, one after the other: hat down over his eyes in the first, standing in front of the river in the next, sleeping in the hammock in the third. His beard and the way he leaned forward, listening. I was trying to capture what he looked like so I'd have it to take back with me. To remember.

The screen door opened in back of me with that soft swishing noise, and the Old Man came out to look over my shoulder. "Oh, Hollis," he said. "Where'd you learn to do that?"

I shook my head.

"Hollis?"

I looked toward the river, green today, a willow hanging over the edge.

He put his hand on my shoulder. "It's a gift," he said, "to draw things the way they are."

I sat very still. No one had ever said anything like that to me before.

"And something else," he said. "You shine through in your drawings."

I looked up at him, really looked at him, not a quick glance that darted away so he couldn't see my eyes. "My name . . . ," I began as he folded himself down on the step next to me. "Hollis Woods is a real place." I shrugged a little. "Holliswood," I said. "One word, I think."

When the Old Man spoke, I jumped. "It's where they found you, as a baby?"

"An hour old," I said in an I-don't-care voice. "No blanket. On a corner. Somewhere." Didn't a baby deserve a blanket? "And just the scrap of paper: CALL HER HOLLIS WOODS."

One day I had gone to see that place. I ran away from one of my houses—tan, green, brick? I circled Queens, on the subway, off the subway, onto the Q2 bus and off the Q2 bus, until I found the spot.

It was winter, bleak, but the houses were pretty. I never did find the woods, though. I tried to picture it in the spring when I had been born, with birds chirping and the sun shining.

Now I saw Steven come into view in the rowboat. "I play hookey," I told the Old Man. "Everyone says I'm tough, they say I'm trouble."

The Old Man made a sound in the back of his throat.

"Steven is a great kid," I said.

The Old Man looked surprised. I waited to hear if he would say anything, but Steven banged the rowboat hard into the rocks along the bank.

The Old Man made another sound. "Watch that, Steven."

"The kingfisher is on the branch downstream," Steven called. So we went down to the boat and climbed in to go have a look.

The Time with Josie

"*O*ver the river and through the woods . . . ," Josie sang one morning at breakfast. It was a late breakfast. We had stayed up most of the night watching an old black-and-white movie.

"To Grandmother's house?" I asked, dropping a cornflake on the table in front of Henry's nose and jumping back as he raised one paw to warn me.

Josie waggled her hand, her head still bent. She was carving my tree figure from a piece of oak, stripping the bark until the underneath showed pale and smooth. The head was there, still unformed, the nose just a slight sharp mark.

Josie saw me looking at it. "A bit at a time,"

she said. "The face last, when I'm sure I know you well enough."

I didn't say anything. Instead, I ran one finger over Henry's back. His eyes were closed, he was purring, and I figured he didn't know it was me.

"Over the river . . . ," Josie began again, rocking in her chair with a pleased look on her face.

Water, I thought. The ocean. We'd been there twice this week. Odd to see the ocean near the end of November. I'd always thought of it as something to see in the summertime. I put the tea mugs in the sink, sprayed water over them, and waited, leaning against the counter as Josie took a cut in the side of the wood and gently blew the shavings away.

She stood up then, ready to go, but instead, she stopped to peer out the window. "Someone's coming."

I glanced out and saw the gray car pulling into her driveway. The mustard woman had come to check up on me.

My own fault, I told myself. Hanging around here today instead of going to school. It was that lingering-cold note. I hadn't been able to resist it.

"It's the wrong time," I sang to Josie.

She smiled at me, singing too. "And the wrong place?"

I reached for her wool hat and scarf and the brown hat with the veil. "Let's go down to the water instead of entertaining," I told her.

We slipped out the back door, moving as quietly as we could; it was a game. We passed through Josie's tree-figure garden, went through the woods and diagonally across the street.

It was a long walk in the cold, and we hadn't stopped for jackets, so we were both shivering by the time we felt the difference in the air, smelled the sharp, sweetish smell of the ocean.

We climbed up onto the pier. The fishing boats were gone this late in the morning. I knew some of them by now, and I could see the two smaller ones somewhere out near the horizon. I kept thinking of that gray car and trying to decide what to do. I bent down and picked up a shell. Its edges were crushed but it had a beautiful color, almost like the sea itself with the sun shining on it.

"A piece of good luck," Josie said.

I slipped it into a pocket of my jeans and nodded. We needed luck.

Josie had moved away from me. I turned and saw her lying on the jetty, holding her hat on with one hand, the loose end of her scarf floating in the water. She wiggled herself down and down until I thought she'd go over; then at last she reached into the mass of foam that had settled around the stanchions of the pier.

A moment later she was up, strands of sea grass clutched in her hand. Several inches long, curled along the edges, they were the color of sand. Josie smiled at me and held them up to my hair. "I thought so," she said, "almost an exact match."

I nodded, realizing she had gathered them for my wood figure. It made me think of the drawing box the Old Man had given me. How often I had held up a pencil to match the color against something.

Was the drawing box still at the house in Branches?

I turned as I heard the sound of a car and of tires bumping along the wooden planks of the pier in back of me: the mustard woman.

She came to a stop about two inches away from us and rolled down the window. "Why aren't you in school?"

"School?" Josie asked, looking confused.

I didn't answer, of course I didn't. I had learned to keep my mouth closed long ago. In my mind I pulled myself into a small knot deep inside and tried to think about something else, anything else.

"Get in the car," the mustard woman said, "I'll drive you there right now."

One of the fishing boats had almost disappeared. All that was left of it was the needle-thin mast on top.

Someday I'd like to be on that boat, I thought, to see what it would be like to look back at the land. I glanced at the railing that ran along the end of the pier. It was so low it would be hard to see from a ship.

"School," Josie said. "Of course." She put her hand on my shoulder. It was the hand holding the sea grass. I felt a soft scratch against my skin.

Josie's legs were bare, with dainty spider veins showing, and her silky shoes were soaked with snow and spray. I didn't want the mustard woman to see them.

I opened the back door of the car and slid in, and we drove off, leaving Josie looking after us, her head tilted as she waved at me, the sea grass in her hand blowing in the wind.

"What's going on here?" the mustard woman said. "No school?"

I ran my tongue over my lips, trying to figure out the best lie I could. "I told her today was a holiday, teachers' conference."

The mustard woman shook her head. "And she believed that?" she said. "We'll have to see about this."

I reached into my pocket and held on to the shell. For the first time in my life, I thought, I'd really have to go to school. I'd have to if I wanted to stay at Josie's.

The Time with Josie

CHAPTER 6

My head was a round burl of wood, the sea grass, dried now, a swirl on top. Josie spent hours over it at the kitchen table, humming to herself, a tray of tiny knives spread out in front of her.

It was Monday, early in December, almost dark in the late afternoon. No Chinese dinner tonight. I was making a dish Izzy had taught me. *"Special deluxe,"* she had said, and smiled at me. Chopped meat, ketchup, Worcestershire sauce, and cheese, spooned over hot rolls. Salad. Pound cake with confectioner's sugar sifted over the top.

It was going to be a special deluxe evening. Beatrice was leaving the next morning for New Mexico, where she'd paint the adobe houses and the desert. "I'll come back when the mood strikes," she had said, "or when my money runs out. We'll close up the movie until I get back."

All week I'd had a pain in my chest. I was waiting to see what the mustard woman would do. School was all right. I kept my head in the books, made As on two tests, and had no friends. But if the mustard woman talked to Josie for more than five minutes she'd know about Josie. Strange, how much I wanted to stay. Maybe it was because Josie needed me. I'd never been needed before. Or wanted? asked a voice in my head. The Old Man had wanted me, I told myself. So had Izzy, so had Steven. Then why?

Don't think about that. Think about Josie.

"A little forgetful," Beatrice had said. "Maybe old age."

But not always forgetful. There was the afternoon Josie had watched me sketch small pictures on my pad. "I remember something." She tapped one red fingernail on her lower lip. "There's paper in the attic. I haven't seen it for years. I think it belonged to my father."

I climbed the stairs; then, bent like a pretzel, I scurried around the low attic, stepping over bags and bushel baskets, stopping to look at boxes of paper-thin Christmas ornaments and yellowed leather gloves, until I found what she'd told me about: huge pieces of paper, gray and dog-eared. I ran my hands over them, thinking about the day the Old Man gave me the drawing box.

As I had maneuvered my way back to the steps, Josie had called up. "There's an easel, too."

Beatrice came now, hurrying up the walk. Her hair had been done up in a high pink swirl at the hairdresser. Her nails matched, and so did her huge pink purse.

We were ready for her with the pound cake on Josie's best plate and the dishes on the table. We ate watching the pale December sun drop behind the trees in the backyard. When Josie went inside for something, Beatrice leaned over. "Take care of her," she whispered.

I thought of telling her about the mustard woman and the agency, but what if Josie came back?

Beatrice saw me frown. "Maybe I shouldn't go."

"Josie said you've wanted to do this all your life."

"But . . ."

"Go," I said, wishing I could go too. I'd take the Shortline bus up through New York State. It would be early summer again, the first time I'd seen Steven and the Old Man, playing checkers in the diner. I'd start over. I'd do everything different.

Everyting.

But instead, I'd do it all right. I'd stay with Josie and . . .

"I'll take care of her," I whispered. Somehow, I said in my head.

Beatrice turned over one of my pictures. "I'll leave my phone number," she said. "I'll write it down." She patted my hand. "I won't be there for the first two or three weeks, I'll be traveling around. But just in case."

I watched her make careful, even numbers on the paper and turn it over as Josie came back into the kitchen, another one of my pictures in her hand.

I didn't take any chances, though. Through the rest of the dinner, I said the phone number over in my head. I wanted to be sure I'd remember it.

Sixth Picture

Driving the Truck

I never showed this picture to anyone: the golden field, me with my head back laughing, my hands at the wheel of the truck. It took four or five pencils to do this: I started with Summer Green, Iron Gray, and Beach Sand. That was something, that Saturday night.

Izzy and the Old Man were going to the movie in town. "It's a romance," the Old Man said, waggling his eyebrows at me. "A waste of a good evening."

"You'll love it, John," Izzy said. "There are snacks in the refrigerator and in the cabinet. Snacks all over the place. You won't starve." She leaned out the door. "And there's a tin of that hard candy on my dresser."

Steven crossed his eyes. "They're so sour they curl your tongue."

"Not mine." I'd been eating them all summer; I couldn't get enough of them.

"That's because—" he began. I knew he was going to joke about my being sour.

But the Old Man came out the door. "I just saw the mess you left in the shed," he told Steven. "Straighten that place up. It's bad enough your room looks the way it does."

"What's this neatness kick?"

"Did you notice how neat Holly's things are?"

Without thinking, I put my hand up. "Don't . . . ," I began, but it came out almost as a breath. Neither one of them heard, or maybe they just weren't paying attention.

Steven unfolded himself from his chair so slowly, it seemed as if he weren't moving.

"Hang in there, Hollis Woods," Steven said as the Old Man stamped around the side of the house and started the car. "We're going to be out of here in five minutes."

"Where?" Already he was running around the side of the house to the shed.

I sat there listening as he threw things around for a few minutes, and then he was back. "I'm going to teach you to drive. Good thing they took the car instead of the truck." He dangled the keys in front of my nose. "Anyone who can keep her things disinfected can drive a truck."

"I don't think—" I began.

"Scared?"

"Never."

"All right, don't waste my valuable time arguing."

In back of the evergreens and the row of holly bushes was a flat field. The Old Man kept it mowed against snakes, rattlers that struck blind in the summer. "Don't worry," Steven said, sliding into the truck. "No one's been bitten for about a hundred years. Pop worries about everything."

Steven drove as if he'd been doing it all his life. He grinned across at me in the suicide seat. "Since I was about eight," he said, knowing what I was thinking. "I'm going to take the truck up the mountain one day."

He showed me the gears and the pedals, and then we switched seats. And so I drove in that field in the summer-evening light, Steven shouting directions as I lurched through the ruts, bucking, stalling, starting up again with gear-grinding noises.

"Aha, Hollis Woods," he yelled. "There's hope for you. I knew it!"

I pressed my foot down on the gas pedal a little harder. "Yahoo!" I yelled. "It's me, driving a pickup truck!"

The Time with Josie

CHAPTER 7

*O*ne raw Tuesday morning I awoke and pulled the shade aside; the trees were charcoal smudges against an iron gray sky. Josie wouldn't be up for another hour or two. I hadn't done my homework the night before, hadn't even thought of it. I'd fallen asleep watching television with Henry next to me on the couch and Josie working at the kitchen table.

I still faced rows of math problems. Three pages, maybe four. And there was a social studies composition on Henry Hudson.

I tried to decide whether I could work on it now. It was early. I popped bread into the toaster and opened a can of Salmon Delight for Henry, who sniffed at it and walked away.

"I can never figure you out," I said, and buttered a square of toast for him instead. Then I pulled my books off the shelf and sat at the table with one of Josie's knitted shawls around me.

In back of me I had the radio on. Two weeks until Christmas. It had snowed upstate, six inches.

Ah, snow for Steven. Were they up yet, the three of them? Were they having breakfast in their winter house in Hancock? What would it be like if I were there, doing my homework, eating Izzy's apple pancakes?

The radio announcer said it was a foggy day on Long Island at three minutes before eight o'clock.

I finished the first page of math problems; I could never do the rest in a half hour. Never mind Henry Hudson sailing up the river.

Maybe I could take one more day off. Just one. I grabbed my jacket and pad and went out the back door, holding it open for Henry to come too. The canal would be wonderful this morning, with a mist rising off the water. And all the while I jogged toward the jetty, I knew it was a mistake. But still I kept going.

When I got to the pier, I sat, hands clenched in my pocket against the cold, my legs dangling, watching the fisherman on the *DanBar-J* gear up to go out for blues. He knew me now, and waved. Last week he'd even dropped a flounder on the bench for me. I had panfried it with a little butter, and Josie had put two dusty pink candles on the table, almost like a party.

Henry had loved his share. He hadn't scratched at me once when I put his plate down in front of him on the radio. "Ah," I had said, pleased with him. "You'd do anything for a handout."

Now I watched the fingers of fog drift over the water while Henry sat nearby, washing one mangy leg. It was the kind of day I loved. I couldn't see the end of the pier, and no one could see me from there. I could hear the fisherman from the *DanBar-J*, though. "Want a job?" he called.

He wasn't thinking about school either.

A job? Why not? There'd be money for cat food, a couple of cans of ravioli. I hadn't had ravioli since the stucco house.

I nodded and found myself hosing down the deck of the *DanBar-J*. As I scrubbed at the dried-on pieces of fish with a wire brush, I spent the money in my mind.

He handed me three crumpled-up bills. I smoothed them out, and then as I gave him a half wave, he reached into his pocket and gave me another dollar.

I couldn't wait to get back to Josie. She'd pat her scarf around her neck and fuss with her hat. We'd sail up and down the aisles of DeMattia's Food Store, picking and choosing: ravioli, and a pink can of shredded tuna for Henry. Maybe some marmalade, too, to have with the English muffins we had left.

I had forgotten all about homework, and school, and even the mustard woman. Henry and I headed home as the fog lifted and the sun appeared behind the trees. It was going to be a beautiful day, a day for a picnic on the rock jetty.

I pulled open the back door and stopped. Above the newscaster's voice on the radio—"Nine-thirty and still snowing in upstate New York"—was the sound of voices in the living room.

Henry heard them too. He scampered back outside to sit on the bench, an irritable look on his skinny face.

I thought about scampering with him. I knew who it must be. But how could I leave Josie alone with her? Instead, I shrugged out of my jacket, put my pad on the table, and lifted my chin as I went toward the front of the house.

The mustard woman sat on the lilac couch, and Josie sat in the chair opposite. They both had cups of coffee in their hands.

Good move, Josie, I thought. Her coffee was great, dark and rich, as the advertisements went.

I nodded at the mustard woman and sank down in the third chair, facing the window, looking out as if something wonderful were going on right there in the front yard.

They talked about old movies and the wonderful colors in the living room; they talked about coffee waking them up, and all the time my heart was pounding. Without looking at the mustard woman's face, I knew she was straining at the conversation, that this wasn't what she wanted to say.

She was wearing sweats. . . . Did she ever wear anything else? I could see a round creamy spot on her chest. She'd spilled her coffee. What was the matter with that woman, anyway?

But Josie looked fine, Josie looked wonderful, with that slash of red across her mouth, a silky green dress that looked like the sea. I knew she was groping, though. She had no idea who the woman sitting across from her was.

At last the mustard woman put down her cup. "Hollis," she said, "I know I'm keeping you from school."

I waved my hand. No problem, lady.

She looked at Josie then. "I think, Mrs. Cahill, that we need to talk about another place for Hollis."

Josie sat up straight. I could see her thin hands on the coffee cup trembling a little; her mouth, too. "Hollis is leaving?"

They both looked at me.

"I've found a family for her," the mustard woman said. "A mother and father with a three-year-old boy and a dog." She kept leaning forward, trying to make me look at her. "I think I remember you like dogs, Hollis."

"Sharks," I said, "and barracudas, not dogs."

"A family would be nice," Josie said.

Too late, I thought.

"But not today," the mustard woman said. "It will be a few days. I'll want Hollis to meet them first. They're not so far from here. You and Mrs. Cahill will be able to visit sometimes, Hollis."

She stood up then. "I'll keep in touch," she said. "Would you like me to drive you to school now?"

I shook my head. "I can walk."

She turned to go.

"By the way," I said. "You have a sticker on the back of that shirt. *X-L.*"

She tried to look over her shoulder.

"Extra large," I said, feeling mean.

Seventh Picture

Izzy

Two of Izzy's candies filled my mouth as I went around the side of the house. I didn't mean to listen or to be sneaky. Ordinarily I did that a lot. I'd stand still in the hall to hear what the stucco woman had to say to her telephone friend. I'd flip pages on the teacher's desk to see what disaster of a mark I'd gotten in social studies or social attitude. I'd pass by classmates in the schoolyard to find out what they had to say about that kid Hollis Woods.

But this time I was on my way to find Izzy, to give her a picture I'd drawn: Izzy flipping a pancake that would land on my plate. Izzy's pancakes were wonderful: covered with apples cut into small sweet chunks, the pancakes themselves so light I must have eaten a half dozen. In the picture Izzy is laughing, the turner in one hand, just under the cross-stitched motto on the wall: LOVE THE COOK.

I'd changed the motto, though. I'd written: I DO LOVE THE COOK. I'd drawn the I DO in the palest pink so that you'd have to study it, study it hard, or you wouldn't notice.

One afternoon Izzy and I had walked up to the old cemetery on the hill where her parents were buried. We picked white daisies and Queen Anne's lace and put them in the jar in front of a small stone next to her parents' grave. Izzy ran her hand over the inscription on the bottom: JOSEPH REGAN, SIX DAYS. "I always wanted more children," she said. "For me, for John, for Steven." She patted the stone. "I wanted a baby for each corner of my house. It just never happened after this."

Down the hill I could hear the Old Man bellow at Steven. "Do they always fight?" I asked. "Or . . ."—I hesitated, trying to sound as if I didn't care, as if it weren't important—"do you think it's because I'm here?"

Izzy grinned at me. "It does seem worse this summer," she said. "But they have to find their own way."

I'd thought about that for days, "worse this summer," but now, as I rounded the house, I *stepped back against the wall, warm from the sun, smelling faintly of paint, and closed my eyes.*

"How can we let her go?" Izzy was saying.

"We can't," the Old Man said.

My heart began to pound so hard I thought it would come through my chest.

A mother, I thought. M.

"She belongs here," Izzy said. "Steven feels it too."

B, belong. G, girl. S, sister. W for want, W for wish, W for Wouldn't it be loverly? My head was spinning.

"I've been thinking about it," Izzy said. "The winter house in town is too small. We'd have to put a room on for her."

I don't need a room. A couch. A sleeping bag.

"Without the room, I don't think the agency would let us keep her. She has to have space for herself."

For a moment they were quiet.

I leaned my head back, my hand to my mouth.

"How about this?" Izzy said. "You could call Lenny Mitchell to work with you. There's space in the back for a great room for Hollis."

"A big window for her," the Old Man said. "We could do it in weeks."

"Sooner than weeks," Izzy said. "Early fall."

"Yes. Even Steven would help."

"I'll call—"

"You'll call the agency."

"How long will it take them?

"She'll have to go back first," Izzy said, the words tumbling over each other.

"But just for a short time."

I leaned my head against the wall. I'd never been so happy.

"A daughter," Izzy said.

"Yes," the Old Man said. "We'll have a daughter."

From where I stood I could see the mountain towering over me. The stucco woman's voice was in my head: "She's a mountain of trouble, that Hollis Woods."

Before the end of the summer, I decided, I was going to climb that mountain, get to the top, raise my arms, and shout to the whole world, "I have a family. I belong."

In back of me there was a noise. "Ya-hoo!"

Steven. I jumped a foot.

The voices stopped, but no one knew I had heard.

Early fall and I'd be a daughter.

The Time with Josie

CHAPTER 8

*F*or the next few afternoons, around five, the mustard woman called to chitchat. That's what she called it. She was doing all the chatting.

"How was school?"

"Burned down."

"What did you have for lunch?"

"Horse meat."

"How's Mrs. Cahill?"

"Who?"

"What are you drawing?"

"Nudies."

"Hollis," she said slowly one night. "Mrs. Cahill is old, and she has a tendency to forget."

Josie dancing in the street, giving me the hat with the veil, making popcorn at the movie.

I said more than I wanted to. "She doesn't forget everything, just some things." I stopped. The mustard woman would never change her mind. I raised my hand to the window. Drops of melting sleet were running down the glass. Under the kitchen table Henry was an orange ball, with only his pointy little chin turned up. Henry hated sleet.

"Tomorrow is Saturday," the mustard woman began. "I'll pick you up and take you to meet Eleanor." She paused.

I didn't answer.

"That's her name, Eleanor. She's going to have lunch for us."

I pulled the telephone cord as far as it would go.

"Then Sunday, if all goes well . . ." She broke off. "You'd be in the same school. And you could visit Mrs. Cahill often."

I took the phone away from my ear and put it on the counter. I did it gently so there was no noise. I wondered how long she'd keep talking before she figured out I wasn't listening.

It was gray outside. Josie's wooden figures were blurred and bent in the wind that had just come up.

Josie couldn't stay alone. She might not remember

when it was supper. She'd sit up all night watching movies.

Beatrice. I picked up the phone and pressed the numbers. It rang about twenty times. *Answer, Beatrice.* But then I remembered. For the first weeks she'd be traveling around, she had said. I pictured her in the desert, dry sun beating down, her sketchbook in her hand.

I couldn't leave Josie.

I couldn't stay.

It was a puzzle.

Something from years ago popped into my head. It wasn't winter, it was summer, and so humid everything I touched was sticky. All afternoon I'd thought about the pillow on the bed, and how cool it would be against my head. I was surprised when it was as hot as the rest of the room. I reached under the pillow to find something I had hidden there, a doll with pale painted eyes. I whispered to her, asking if she was cooling off. And then someone came and pulled her away, tossing her on the night table. I waited until the woman walked out the door, and then I whispered a little more loudly so that the doll could hear me. "Don't worry," I'd said. "I'll save you in the morning."

Why had I thought of that now?

Save Josie.

That's why.

The sleet outside was turning to snow. It reminded me of Steven. *"You'd love the snow in Hancock,"* he'd said.

I thought of the summer house in Branches. *"I haven't been here in winter since I was a boy,"* the Old Man had said. *"But it was wonderful, so cold it hurt your teeth, the river frozen over, the animals coming up close to the house. Everything was silver with ice."* He had spread his wide hands. *"Twisted icicles this long hanging from the roof. I used to knock them off and see how far I could throw them."* He had laughed. *"My father had put in heat, so when you came inside, it was warm. I'd dry my hands on the radiator till they almost sizzled."*

Winter.

No one there in the house in Branches. *"We stay in our house in Hancock now. Plenty of snow there, and nearer to school and the stores."*

How could I do it?

How could I not?

Josie was napping on the lilac couch. I went in and stood next to her, watching that beautiful face.

She opened her eyes.

"How would you like to go away with me?" I asked.

"To see Beatrice?" she said.

I shook my head. "That's too far."

"Then where?" She sat up, smoothing her hair with papery thin fingers.

It was hard to get the words out. "We'll take the car."

"The Silver Bullet," she said, nodding.

"It will be an adventure," I said.

She smiled. "Henry, you, and I in the Silver Bullet. We'll fly to the ends of the earth."

I smiled back, trying to think. Food, warm clothes, gas for the Silver Bullet.

It was Friday night. The mustard woman would come for me at lunchtime tomorrow.

By then we had to be long gone.

Eighth Picture

End of Summer

We were frenzied that last week in August. That was Izzy's word: frenzied. *And I drew it all:*

Steven and I racing along the dirt road to buy beef jerky at the grocery store four miles away.

Sitting on a rock, pulling the jerky against our teeth as we counted the cars that went by on the highway.

Rowing up the river rapids and bouncing back in the rowboat with bruises all over our legs and arms.

Climbing partway up the Old Man's mountain after the rain, slipping and sliding in the mud on the edge of the road.

And we never stopped laughing.

Anything so we wouldn't think about my leaving.

Anyting.

They told me what they'd planned, the four of

us sitting on the porch. I never needed a picture of that night. It was in my head, every bit of it, in there forever. But I drew it anyway: Izzy with one of my hands in both of hers, the Old Man reaching out to hug me until I had no breath left, and Steven blinking behind his glasses, trying not to let me see how close to tears he was. But I knew.

I drew another picture of what happened next. Before I could think, I leaned over to kiss Steven's cheek, stained with grease from working on the truck, captured there in that drawing forever. Both of us laughed, embarrassed, and Izzy said, "Lovely. I'm going to try that too." And she leaned over to kiss his other cheek.

We were still laughing as Izzy spread out her long arms. "It's settled, then," she said. "You belong with us. This house . . ."

"And the river," I said.

". . . is yours," the Old Man said. "All of it."

"And Izzy's hard candy," Steven said, rocking back on his chair, looking happier than he had all summer.

Please let it be all right, I begged, looking at Steven's face, remembering all the arguments he and the Old Man had had: a lost lure yesterday, a rake left in the rain, the truck. Was it because I was there? Was the Old Man comparing him with me?

Me? *Wasn't that strange? Was trying to fit me into a family like jamming in a puzzle piece that didn't match? Would it ruin all the other pieces?*

I looked up at the mountain. The trees had just a hint of fall color. The mountain looked soft, almost friendly. I thought about standing on the very top.

Izzy leaned over. *"Hey, you two, don't look sad. We still have one last weekend. Remember?"*

The last weekend.

Last.

The Time with Josie

CHAPTER 9

*N*ever mind that we didn't have much money. Never mind that I didn't even know exactly how to get to the house in Branches; I'd find it. Never mind that the house wasn't mine.

Please don't mind, I said to Izzy and the Old Man in my head.

I ticked off what to pack, what to do, counting on my fingers: Bring all the food in the cabinet over the sink, a map, winter clothes, piles of anything warm I could find in the house, then get gas at the first exit off the highway.

Josie was in the kitchen making cocoa. "It'll be dark soon," she said.

"That's all right," I told her. "We like the dark. It's like velvet."

"That it is," she said. "And we like the snow, too."

I bit my lip. Dark and snow. One problem after another.

"How about marshmallows in our cocoa?" Josie asked.

"Left-hand cabinet," I said.

To begin with, Josie and I had to get off Long Island, I knew that; we had to get to Route Seventeen and exit at Ninety, and after that we were home free. I had walked that last few miles dozens of times: the grocery store off the ramp, the road curving over the hill. We'd cross the bridge and the house would be there, nestled in the trees opposite the Old Man's mountain.

I could do it in my sleep.

I called back over my shoulder, reminding Josie where we were going: "It's a house in the woods, Josie," I said. "A house on the river, a safe house."

I swept half boxes of cereal off the counter into a carton, cans of chicken noodle soup, sugar, salt, anything I could find to eat, then, wasting precious time, went up to the attic for Josie's old Christmas ornaments.

I heard a car and froze on the top step. The sound of the motor grew louder and then gradually disappeared. My heart was beating fast.

Stop, I told myself. The mustard woman was far away, in her house somewhere, scarfing up her dinner, littering her sweat suit with crumbs.

But I knew we should leave as quickly as we could. I'd learned that when I'd run before. The first hours made all the difference, the hours before anyone knew you were gone.

I scurried into the attic, found the box of ornaments, and pulled it after me to the stairs.

When I finished, the car was piled so high it was hard to see out the windows. It was completely dark now, except for the white flakes hitting the window. In the kitchen Josie was bent over the table, a cup of cocoa in one hand, her knife in the other, and the smooth chunk of wood in front of her.

"Josie?" I reached out for my own cup of cocoa and sipped at it, feeling the warmth of it on my lip, the sweetness of the marshmallow in my mouth. I touched her shoulder. "We can't wait anymore."

Rubbing her eyes, she glanced toward her bedroom. I knew she wanted to take a nap. I did too; I was tired now, and thinking of the long trip ahead of us was almost too much.

"We'll have an adventure," I said. "You, and me, and Henry." I hesitated. "If we don't go, they might make me live somewhere else."

She stood up. "We'll go, then." She looked around

at the kitchen, touched the table, the back of the chair. "Yes," she said. "We'll go."

"Can you drive?" I asked.

Please let the snow stop, I thought.

She smiled. "Of course."

I made one last trip to the car, carrying her knives, the small drill, pieces of wood, and then I was back, hoisting Henry onto my shoulder. "No biting, if you don't mind," I told him.

We went outside, Josie looking up at the sky, holding out her hands to catch the flakes while I opened the garage doors, and then we were off, skidding our way down the street.

Suddenly the snow did stop, and we saw a moon over our heads. "It looks dusty," Josie said. The houses stood out as clearly as if it were daytime; trees threw sharp shadows across the snowy lawns, and the dark streets curved like ribbons through that white world. I put my head back against the headrest, thinking we'd done it. The hardest part was over.

"Do you know about directions?" I asked.

She turned her head to one side. "It depends. I know the way to the end of Long Island, I know how to get upstate. . . ."

"Upstate, yes."

"Across the Triborough Bridge." She frowned, looking worried. "Isn't that right?"

"I think so." Harry was scratching around in back, trying to make room for himself.

"There's a map somewhere." Josie leaned across me, one hand off the wheel.

"I can find it," I said quickly, reaching for the glove compartment. A tiny pinprick of light appeared as I snapped it open. The small space inside was filled with all kinds of things: one of Josie's silk gloves, a couple of dimes, a squished box of tissues, and at the very bottom, the map of New York State.

I unfolded it, spreading it out against the door of the glove compartment. It was a mass of color and lines and tiny words that were hard to see in that dim light. I bent over it, squinting. *Palisades Parkway. Route 17.* It was all there, one line after another, leading me home to Branches.

I looked up as I heard the blare of a horn, and then a car swerved past us, its lights sweeping over the road. "Are you all right?" I asked Josie.

"Right as rain," she said.

I sat back and closed my eyes, thinking of Izzy, drawing them all in my mind, wondering if they'd think I was doing a terrible thing.

"It belongs to you," the Old Man had said. Would he say that now? I wondered.

Why not? said Steven in my mind.

Izzy's face in front of mine. Would she say, *"Do it, Hollis"*? I thought she would.

I was doing it anyway.

Suddenly I sat up straight. How much gas did we have? It was almost a miracle to see the Mobil sign off to the right. I touched Josie's arm, pointing, and we pulled off the road, waiting for the attendant to fill the tank while I counted out my running money.

"Good idea," Josie said, and I had to smile at her. She'd have driven until the tank was empty, and might never have remembered.

I was hungry now, really hungry. The hot chocolate hadn't lasted long. And I hadn't had lunch. Maybe I could hurry inside for a bag of potato chips and a chocolate bar. I glanced out the rearview mirror to see a car pulling up in back of us at the pump. The man was impatient, tapping his horn for us to get out of the way. There'd be no time to buy anything, not even enough time to rummage through the back to find the bags of food.

I thought of the mustard woman. She'd come up the path tomorrow afternoon to get me, trying to smile, acting as if this would be a lovely afternoon tea at that woman's house—what was her name? Eleanor. When we didn't answer the bell, maybe she'd go around the back to see if we were in Josie's garden.

But soon enough she'd figure out that we weren't there. She'd stand on tiptoe to look in the window of the garage, and it would be empty. If we were lucky, she'd wait awhile. She might think we'd be back any minute. But the minutes would stretch out to an hour, and then she'd know. She'd really know. And then she'd call the police.

My hands were damp.

Calm down, I made Steven tell me in my mind. *You knew all this before you started.*

But Josie turned onto the parkway now, and it wouldn't be that long before we crossed the bridge and left Long Island, maybe twenty minutes, and the mustard woman would just be getting ready for bed.

Next to me, in the dim light, I couldn't see the lines around Josie's eyes, or the ones crisscrossing her forehead. I could pretend we were taking a moonlight ride in the Silver Bullet, pretend Josie was all right and we weren't running.

The last time I had run was two weeks after what had happened in Branches. It was September, still hot, with the sun beating down from early morning until dark. It was hard to move, hard to think; everything hurt in my head and my chest. I'd had enough of the stucco woman and I knew she'd had enough of me. All I could think about was being somewhere cold, a place where I could scoop up a chunk of snow and crush it against my teeth, a place to make the heat and the pain go away.

I left at night, after the stucco woman had fallen asleep. It gave me hours to get out on the road, to find a bus. I was gone for days before they caught me.

Maybe we'd be luckier this time.

The Time with Josie

CHAPTER 10

*I*t was late when we reached the exit sign for Branches. The gas station light was out, and there was only a tiny light in the back of the grocery store. "We're almost there," I told Josie, "just the last four miles."

"Already?" She sounded delighted. She zoomed off the ramp, stopping on the shoulder, and in a moment she was asleep, her head against the steering wheel. Henry climbed off my lap, where he'd been for the past hour, and slid onto hers, his whiskers twitching as he closed his eyes.

I leaned over and turned the key to stop the motor. Suddenly I was wide awake and reaching for the door handle. I gave Henry a pat, then I got out of the car.

At first it was hard to see, but little by little silhou-ettes appeared against the sky: the curve of a tree trunk, the dark square of the grocery store ahead, and above us, the Old Man's mountain, raising its head to the sky. It was almost a shock to see it there.

Beatrice would have said it was a drawing coming to life. I pictured her in a place with huge cacti, saguaro, I thought they were called. I remembered she'd said she would call every Sunday. What would she think when the phone rang and rang?

I shook myself. What would happen if I tried to call her again?

She'd come home, her dream over.

I wasn't going to do that. Back in the car, I nudged Josie awake. "Just drive this last bit," I said, "and then you can sleep."

We drove along the narrow road, no other lights now except for a few houses far up on the hills, and I kept talking to keep her awake. "We'll see the river. It's not as big as your ocean. . . ."

"Your river." Josie's head bobbed.

"Keep watching," I told her. "We don't want to go off the road. The river would be cold for a swim."

I saw her smile. "Henry doesn't have his bathing suit."

And there was the bridge. I had stood on that bridge watching the pickerel, the catfish, the muskrat building his nest of sticks against its base.

The Old Man's bridge.

"We'll have a fire in the fireplace," I said, "and turn the heat up high." I could see the Old Man flipping the switch in the early mornings when dew was still on the grass and the house was still cold.

We thumped across the bridge over the river, and the house was in front of us, waiting. "Josie, this is the place." My voice was flat. I might have been telling her it was a snowy day or the sun might come out tomorrow, but inside, my heart was thumping.

We had just this winter, I knew that, and maybe the spring. By summer we'd have to find somewhere else.

That was months. That was forever.

I closed my eyes, remembering the last morning I had been here. I had gone out the screen door toward the car, brushing my fingers along the holly bushes, feeling the sharp edges of the leaves against my thumb.

I had walked as far as the town, a long way in the early-morning heat, and sat on the bench with my things on my lap, waiting for the Shortline bus, and looking down, I realized I'd left the drawing box. I think that was the worst moment, knowing I'd never see that box again. Geranium Red, Dove Gray, French Blue.

"We're home, Josie," I said.

"Hard to see," she said.

"Just get used to the darkness," I told her. "In a minute you'll see it all."

She took everything in then, and I with her: the house with the sloping roof, the evergreens leaning over it, the dark shadow that was the woodpile on the front porch. The rocking chairs were in the shed, I knew that, but I could picture them there, rocking gently.

Josie took a deep breath.

"I knew you'd like it," I said, watching Henry in the rearview mirror. He stood on the back of the headrest now, his claws in my shoulder, his nose twitching, his whiskers quivering, sizing up the place. "And you too, Henry."

"But is it all right?" Josie asked, frowning. "Are you sure we can do this?"

"We can." I brushed away thoughts of being caught, of what the Old Man might think of me if he ever found out. What did he think of me anyway? *Please don't mind this thing I'm doing,* I begged him in my head.

A red cardinal swooped down to perch on a holly branch that bent itself into the snow, snow marked by threadlike bird prints and deep hollows from the deer. The tracks hugged the edge of the clearing, close to the evergreens, and one path, probably from a rabbit, led to the river.

I wondered if Steven had ever seen the house in the winter. He would love it.

I chewed my knuckle. A lace curtain of snow blew across the porch. It was bitter cold with the engine turned off. I had to get Josie into the house. Her shoes had heels, with open toes and diamond-shaped cutouts in the sides. Why hadn't I thought of her shoes?

Henry scratched his claws along the car window, wanting to get out. I gave his ear a tweak, opened the door, and watched him belly through the snow away from the car.

"I'm sorry, Josie," I said, still looking down at her feet. They'd be soaked. "You'll have to walk through this to get to the house."

"An adventure," Josie said, grabbing the handle.

I slipped her scarf up around her head, the orange a bright spot in the darkness, and buttoned the top button of her coat. "All right," I said.

Outside we skirted the trees, and she stopped to look up. "A million stars," she said, pointing. "There's the Dipper and Orion. Beatrice would love it." Then I held her by the waist as we went up the back steps.

Her face was a little disapproving as I kicked my sneaker off and, hopping, smashed in the small kitchen window. And then we were inside, Henry skittering in around us.

I leaned back against the wall, reaching for the light, hoping they hadn't turned off the electricity. Suddenly the kitchen sprang to life. The refrigerator began to hum, and beyond it, I could see the huge living room with the long table at one end and dark blue rugs scattered across the wood floor. The Old Man was proud of that floor; he always talked about putting it in with Izzy, about matching the pieces of wood exactly, holding up his hands as if Steven and I could see them clutching a hammer and saw.

Josie shivered, her lips colorless, and my hands felt numb. I flipped the switch for heat and heard the furnace start up. At the fireplace chunks of wood and paper were piled in a bin. I knelt there, crumpling the yellowed newspapers to tuck in between some logs, and read last summer's news as I struck a match against the stones of the hearth: Someone had caught a huge trout near Byron's Falls; a sidewalk sale was planned for Main Street; there were canoes for rent in Shadyside.

I had been here last summer; all of that had been happening. I kept talking to Josie, telling her that this place had been mine only for a month or two, but now it was ours. And she sank down on the couch, nodding, watching the fire.

Is it still mine? I asked the Old Man. *Mine for just this winter?*

A thin flame curled up from somewhere underneath the logs and Josie clapped her hands. "Fire!"

The Old Man's wooden floor shone with a rosy gleam, and my eyes began to close as my fingers warmed, but I couldn't fall asleep yet.

I settled Josie on the couch and found an old towel to dry her feet. They were mottled from the cold. "Skinny as a bird," I told her as I rubbed them. She put her head back, asleep again.

In the kitchen I used the same towel to close the opening in the missing window pane. While we were here I'd figure out how to replace that. There was glass in the shed; I'd seen the Old Man measuring and cutting.

I climbed the stairs to the little green room that had been mine. Everything was just the same. The dresser mirror reflected my old sneakers, just visible under the edge of the bumpy white bedspread; the curtains, pink with roses, looped back; and the drawing box on the dresser.

The drawing box.

I ran my fingers over that half-opened box, the pencils spilling out: French Blue, Geranium Red. It was hard to swallow. I touched all of the pencils, the pad of paper, the sharpener.

Henry and I made four or five trips back to the car for things I had taken from Josie's house. Steam came from my mouth in small white puffs and from the chimney in larger ones. But the cold didn't bother Henry. He pranced through the snow, chasing twigs and a few crumpled leaves as if he were a kitten. He must have known what I was thinking. He sneaked a look back at me; then he sat up on a rock, perfectly still, like the old cat he was.

I'd draw that later, I thought, Henry happy in the dark, with the river just a thread curving through the snow.

It took a half hour to bring everything inside. I wrapped a blanket around Josie, and through the window I could see the car at the edge of the road. There'd be room for it in the shed, I thought, remembering the Old Man's car on one side, the truck on the other.

The truck. Totaled. Was it still there? I shook my head. "I'll be back," I said to the sleeping Josie. "I have to put the Silver Bullet in the shed."

You're going to drive it in? Steven asked in my head.

You taught me how, I said.

But . . .

I can do this.

The truck hugged one side of the shed. I walked around to the front of it and ran my fingers over the cold metal, the sharp edges, the empty holes where the lights had been. I raised my hands to my ears without thinking so I wouldn't hear the sound of the truck as it hit the trees that summer evening.

Outside a few minutes later, I turned the key in the Silver Bullet's ignition; the gas gauge was hitting Empty. Just one more bit, I begged the car, that's all I need. I sat there hesitating before I put my foot on the gas, but then I coasted along over the snow, the motor coughing, and glided into the shed—not touching the sides, not even close—braked a split second before I hit the back wall, and turned off the motor.

Ah, Steven said.

It was quiet, with only the soft whoosh of wind and the muffled sound of icy snow as it blew against the roof. I had done it. All I wanted to do now was curl up under the covers in that small green room upstairs and sleep.

Ninth Picture

Izzy's Cake

I have this drawing folded carefully in my backpack. We're sitting at the table on the porch, the river in front of us, a summer rain drilling the roof above us, soaking us all that last Saturday, muddying the road, greening the grass, puckering the river.

In the picture Izzy is backing out of the screen door, balancing the cake plate in her hands. The cake was vanilla, and Izzy had gathered blue forget-me-nots to circle it.

I used the sharpest pencil (Strawberry Pink) to write the words on top of the cake: WELCOME TO THE FAMILY, HOLLY.

Izzy frowned. "I wanted to get your whole name in, but there wasn't enough room."

The Old Man's eyes sparkled. A moment before I framed the picture in my mind, he patted my shoulder. "Hollis Woods, with us forever."

Steven sat on the other side. I'd drawn pages of animal tracks for him, raccoon and deer, rabbit and possum . . . and birds, even a loon that had come up out of the water to sun itself on a rock.

"I'll probably keep them forever, Sister Loon," he said, full of himself. "Get it?" He pointed to the loon tracks on the side of the page, nudging me under the table like a six-year-old, rattling the glasses, the cake plates.

"Steven, please." The Old Man hadn't been happy with him all week. Nothing gigantic; little stuff. Steven had left the shed door open, so a raccoon had nested inside . . . probably the one whose toes were marching all over Steven's paper. Steven had left the house door open, so a bat had flown around the living room Wednesday night. He'd lost the Old Man's fishing knife, and one of the reels was probably sunk under the water somewhere downstream.

"Why don't you just try with him?" I had asked Steven the day before as we rowed around looking for it.

I could see the anger in his eyes. "You're good enough for both of us," he had said. "That's what Pop would say."

I leaned forward. "Is it me?" I asked. "My fault?"

He had laughed then. "Don't be silly."

Still, I wasn't sure. I opened my mouth to tell him about me, a mountain of trouble, but before I could, he tapped my arm. "Hey." His eyes were earnest behind his glasses. "You don't have to look like that." He broke off a piece of holly and handed it to me. "Peace, Hollis. It's just like you. Prickly, but not bad to look at."

I had tried to hide my smile.

Now Izzy put the cake in the center of the table. "Should we have candles?" she asked.

"Sure." Steven grinned at me. "The works."

"Why not?" I leaned back. I was full of myself too, thinking about calling the Old Man Pop, and Izzy Mom.

Izzy went inside to rummage through the table drawers for the candles, and Steven turned to me, saying we might walk up on the mountain after supper.

The Old Man looked at him sharply. "In the rain?"

"Don't worry." I knew I could make the Old Man smile. "We're tougher than the rain."

"I'm not talking about going all the way to the top," Steven said.

We ate the cake then, the icing melting on my tongue, and I was feeling guilty because I was *really the one who wanted to go up on the mountaintop.*

The end of the old Hollis. Hey, world, here comes the new one.

And I wanted to go alone.

The Time with Josie

CHAPTER 11

*T*he next afternoon I went from room to room, taking my time, looking at everything. Almost everything. I didn't go into Izzy and the Old Man's bedroom. That was their private place.

Photographs filled the guest room wall, and I spent a long time looking at each one. I waited to get to the end to see if the one of me was still there.

First there was a young Izzy in a two-piece bathing suit, then the Old Man sawing down a dead tree, sawdust coloring his beard. There were several of Steven: one without his front teeth, in a bunny costume, one sitting on the hood of the truck, and one with the fishnet in his hand, his head thrown back, laughing.

And the one of me was still there. I was sharpening

a pencil, with pale pink shavings falling in a pile on my drawing paper. I ran my finger over it: still there, in the row with the others, still belonging with them.

Steven's room was next, a mess of a room. Socks on the floor, a jumble of string, a couple of keys, and a photo on the dresser. A photo I couldn't even make out, blurs of greens and blues, and something in the center that might have been the boat.

Behind me Josie called, "I found boots. I'm going to wear them."

"It's too cold to go out," I called back. "You'll freeze." But the outside door slammed, and I went to the window. "Josie?" I put my hand on the glass; cold air drifted in around the panes.

Josie was wearing Izzy's wading boots, which went up to her thighs. She twirled in the snow, arms out, fingers spread. It made me dizzy to watch her. After a moment she tipped over, but it was an easy fall, making me think of snow angels. Her scarf blew across the smooth whiteness, a scrap of color.

She was up again, zigzagging, and I thought about going after her as she disappeared in back of the line of evergreens. I hurried a little, grabbing my jacket. The thermometer outside the kitchen window read five degrees, and next to the window, on the wall, the calendar was still at August.

August.

I went out the back door, calling to her. And then in that cold stillness I could hear her singing. "Over the river . . ."

I went after her, my feet heavy, twirling as I passed the circle she had made, singing back, ". . . and through the woods . . ."

She leaned against a small tree, staring at the thin strip of dark water that ran between the chunks of ice. "Isn't it beautiful?" I said.

"I love to walk in the snow." She was shivering again, looking up at me, suddenly bewildered. "But why aren't we home? And what happened to Beatrice?"

I led her back into the house, into that warm room with the bright blue rugs and the huge couch. I found a robe of Izzy's and wrapped it around her. We sat by the fireplace watching the shadows dance over the walls until it grew dark outside and we slept.

In the morning points of light danced over my eyes. I raised my hand to my face; sun was melting tiny swirls of ice on the window.

Somewhere outside was a faint buzzing sound. It wasn't close—nothing to worry about—but what was it? Someone using a saw deep in the woods? A snowmobile? The sound gradually died away, and I stood up slowly, thinking about breakfast. There were choices, thanks to Izzy: cans of pineapple juice, blackberry jam, vegetables shiny inside their glass jars, rows of Dinty Moore stew.

Izzy's treasures, not mine.

I'd pay her back someday, I told myself, pay back all of it.

Lighten up, Steven said in my head. I had to smile. That's really what he would have said.

I unclenched my hands and took another look outside. Footprints crisscrossed the snow. Our footprints. I thought about them uneasily, glancing up at the sky, wishing for more snow to hide them.

I put water on to boil and popped a piece of Josie's bread into the toaster. A mouse lived somewhere in the house. Poor mouse. He'd have to leave now that Henry was here. I wiped away the mouse's leavings with a brush, then sat at the table in front of the window, with Josie's wood pieces on one side and my food lined up in front of me.

After I ate I looked at the tree figure Josie was doing of me: a long piece of wood, spaces drilled in the sides where the arms would be, a face beginning to take shape, a mouth begun, a small, pointed nose, and a tiny cut on the forehead.

I put my hand up to my own forehead, feeling that indentation. And then Josie was there, yawning, her hair a whoosh around her head. She pattered over to the back window. "Sun today," she said, holding her hands out as if to warm them against the glass. "And a branch that's blown onto the step. Holly, I think."

I took the last bit of toast crust and crunched it into my mouth.

"The sun on the ocean makes a path sometimes." Josie reached for a chocolate bar. "You think you can walk on it, walk clear across the ocean to . . ."

She stopped and I tried to help her. "To England? To France?"

"To where I belong." She sat at the table and began to work. As I put toast and hot tea in front of her, she glanced around.

"What?" I asked.

"I'm wondering about Beatrice," she said, and smiled. "And sandpaper. Your face needs smoothing."

There might be sandpaper in the shed. I'd get it. I didn't have to look at the truck again; I'd pretend it wasn't there. I opened the back door to a blast of cold air— *"So cold your teeth hurt,"* the Old Man had said— and saw the holly branch, thick with bright red berries, that had blown across the steps.

Steven holding a sprig of holly out to me: *"Peace, Holly."*

"I'll get my jacket," I told Josie. I shrugged into it, pulled on my gloves, and went outside for the sandpaper. The cold went through me, the smell of it sharp and clean.

The mustard woman was far away, probably looking for me. She wouldn't have a clue.

On the way back, I bent down and picked up the holly to bring into the house. I gave Josie the squares of sandpaper, then put the branch in one of Izzy's vases in front of the big window, thinking about Christmas. Maybe ten more days.

Josie and I would have our own. I'd cut boughs of pine, and we had packs of popcorn to make. It would be like Christmas in a book by Laura Ingalls Wilder.

I was happier than I had been anywhere, except . . .

. . . I didn't belong in that house in Branches, not anymore. I wondered what Christmas was like in the Old Man's winter house, what it would be like this year.

I snipped off that thought before I finished it. Wasn't it enough that I was here in Branches, with holly in the window?

If only I could stay forever.

Something else the Old Man had told me about: fishing in the winter. The fish went deep, but if you caught one, the eating was an experience.

An experience. The Old Man used words like that.

Fish for dinner, dotted with butter . . . No butter. Ah, fish smothered in tomato sauce, and string beans jarred last summer. A real meal, the way normal people ate. Better than normal.

"I know you like fish," I said to Josie.

"Goldfish. I had one in a bowl, I think." She glanced at Henry, who slept in the middle of one of the Old Man's blue rugs. "I don't trust Henry, though."

"To eat, I mean, for us."

She looked across at me, shocked. "I'd never eat a goldfish."

I could feel the laughter bubble up. "Pickerel," I said. "Bass. I'm not sure what's around this time of the year."

"Ah, yes." She picked up her knife to shave curly bits off the wooden feet.

The Old Man's fishing equipment was hanging on the far wall. Did I really want to go out into that icy world? Of course I did. In Steven's bedroom I gathered things to keep warm: his old green sweater for a scarf around my neck, an extra pair of socks. I found a towel in the hall closet to wrap around my head like a turban, and one of Izzy's large sweaters to put over the whole thing.

I was ready with the pole in my hand. Josie laughed at the sight of me as I passed her.

"The abominable snowman," I said, and then I was outside, trying to decide. I could fish from the bank or the Old Man's bridge. The bank was closer, so I walked along the tree line and down to a spot almost in front of the house. I swung the pole, lure on the line, over the ice into the narrow stream of water. I didn't know how long I stood there fishing, but after a while I leaned back against a bare maple tree, watching movement on the other side of the river, just the quickest bit of color. A squirrel? A raccoon? But then I saw it was something larger, maybe a deer.

It took one more moment to realize that a person, maybe a fisherman, was standing there, back among the trees. And if I had seen him, he might be able to see me.

The pole slid out of my hands as I lurched backward toward the holly bushes. Another quick step and Steven's sweater pulled away on a branch. I looked back to see the pole on the snowy bank. It had sunk into the snow so that it couldn't be seen. There was just a narrow indentation in the snow; it might have been only a branch if anyone spotted it.

My mouth was dry. I looked across the river again. There was no movement on the other side: a scoop of snow slid off one of the branches; a blue jay teetered on another.

I turned and ran the last few steps toward the house and up onto the porch. I reached for the door, closed and locked it in back of me, leaned against it inside, taking deep breaths.

"What is it?" Josie asked.

I shook my head. "Maybe another fisherman. Don't worry." Christmas was coming. Maybe it was someone cutting down a tree, or poaching in the Old Man's woods.

All right. It was all right.

He hadn't seen me, and we were safe.

Josie put on her scarf and her coat and wandered outside, "To breathe for a moment," she told me.

I stayed near the window, watching. But there wasn't anyone there, no one there at all.

Tenth Picture

Hollis Woods

I know what people mean when they say they feel as if they're floating. That's the way I felt, as if my feet weren't attached to the ground, as if they were bouncing off the floor, touching lightly, and bouncing again. And inside me, it was as if bubbles were drifting, bumping gently into each other.

I was happy. No, that doesn't even describe it. I was . . . jubilant, ecstatic.

I drew it using all the pencils—yellows and oranges, pinks and blues. I drew purple shoes on my feet and wings on my shoulders. My eyes were closed, the way you see pictures of angels sometimes with their eyelashes down on their cheeks.

So does it make sense that I wasn't thinking? That all that floating and all those bubbles made me think I could do anything?

And so that last week, all I thought about was going to the top of the Old Man's mountain and shouting down to the whole world. I even knew what I was going to say: Here I am, Hollis Woods, who didn't deserve to be in a family . . . tough Hollis Woods, running-away Hollis Woods. Look at me. I climbed the mountain. Now I belong.

The Time with Josie

CHAPTER 12

*H*alf awake one morning, I heard the sound of a train. I looked up at the window to see a solid square of white: a storm, with pin dots of flakes covering everything. What I had heard was the roar of the wind coming down the valley.

I padded out of bed and went downstairs to see what was happening outside the big window. The holly bushes on one side of the house were just a blur; the narrow sliver of river and its snowy bank had disappeared in a mist of gray.

A little cold, I hugged myself, watching that world. It was like a plastic globe in one of the houses I'd been in. When I shook it, snow fell, covering a bright green Christmas tree in its center.

"Don't touch that, Hollis. Put it down."

I rolled a huge piece of wood onto the banked fire, thinking I'd have to drag more in from the porch later.

Henry looked up at me, meowing, waiting to go out. I reached for the knob, pulling, and when the door opened, a gust of wind blew a swirl of snow inside. Henry stared at me angrily. "Not my fault," I told him, pushing the door closed again.

He went back to the couch, skinny tail twitching.

"Sorry, cat." I ran my hand over the top of his head as I went into the kitchen to rummage through the cabinets.

Ah, how far away the mustard woman was, locked in her house somewhere. How far away everyone was.

I thought of the Old Man, and Steven, and Izzy. They were just a few miles away, but those few miles were forever. Did Steven like the snow, or were they so used to storms like this that they never paid attention to them? I wondered if they ever thought about me the way I did about them. I wondered how Steven was now.

I could hear the Old Man's voice in my ears. I closed my eyes. Don't think of that, don't ever think of that terrible afternoon again.

I took out the box of cocoa with marshmallows and boiled a pot of water on the stove, thinking of what I'd do today. Draw in front of that big window, I told myself. Figure out a way to shade in that soft line of trees, the gray ribbon of river. Charcoal would be wonderful for that; maybe I'd even be able to use a chunk of burned wood from the fireplace.

I'd done other pictures in the past few days and taped them up around the living room: a snowshoe rabbit with his tall ears, four deer nibbling at the bark of the evergreen, the bridge covered in clear ice. I'd done a few of Josie in the snow too, almost nothing but a few quick lines. She walked every day, down to the road, around the evergreens, coming back with her scarf blowing around her face.

What would happen if I left those pictures when we had to leave next spring? What would the Old Man say when he found them?

What would Izzy say? And Steven?

Spring. Could I call Beatrice then? She would have had months. What would happen to me?

Who cared? I'd think of something. But I'd never leave the pictures. I'd take them with me in my backpack.

Sitting at the table, waiting for the cocoa to cool, I thought about Christmas. I'd lost track of the days. I flipped Izzy's wall calendar ahead to December, trying to figure it out. How long had we been here? Eight days? Nine? I counted back.

The water was ready. I mixed the cocoa and took a tiny sip, feeling the heat of it, the steam on my upper lip. Today could be Christmas Eve.

I stood there planning. When the snow stopped, I'd get myself outside and take some of the evergreen branches; there were so many trees we could fill rooms with them. We'd trim the mantel with great heaps of green and tuck Josie's ornaments in among the needles. Maybe we'd find a few pinecones too. We'd have a special dinner tomorrow night. Fruit cocktail and canned tuna, a feast. And popcorn.

I wished I had a present for Josie. The only thing I could give her was a picture of herself. But the more I thought about it, the more I liked the idea. I'd do that today instead of drawing trees. I took another sip of cocoa. What about Josie with Beatrice at the movies in front of their popcorn machine? Both of them would be eating, mouths full, arm in arm, smiling.

"Sleigh bells ring," Josie sang, coming into the kitchen behind me.

"I was just thinking that." I reached for another cup and poured in water for cocoa.

She stopped to peer out the window. "I've watched it snow on the ocean," she said. "It melts as it hits the water." She touched the glass with all five fingers. "There is nothing like the ocean."

I tried to think of something to change the look in her eyes. "I was thinking we'd have a party," I told her, "with your ornaments and tree branches from outside."

She smiled, looking up at the ceiling. "We could listen to carols on the radio," she said. "That's what Beatrice and I do every year—that and talk about when we were young. Where is Beatrice?"

"Painting," I said. "It's warm where she is."

Josie shook her head. "We always make almond cookies; we eat half and sell the other half at the movie."

"It would be nice if we had a radio." I popped two of our last pieces of bread into the toaster. "And too bad we don't have a few eggs around."

"Or almond syrup," she said.

"Or butter," I said, and we both laughed.

"We'd have to ask Santa Claus," she said. "He'd bring it all to us on his . . ." She paused, thinking.

"Sleigh."

She shook her head. "That was a hundred years ago. Now he comes on a . . ." She looked up at the ceiling.

I laughed. "A motorbike?"

"One of those snow things." She nodded, laughing too. "But how could we not have a radio? Everyone has a radio."

I finished off my cocoa, one sweet marshmallow left in my mouth, trying to remember. Had there been a radio here? There was never television, I remembered that. But Josie was right, there must be a radio. I wandered around, searching, and finally found one on a shelf, behind boxes of old jigsaw puzzles, the old cord wrapped around it. All that time Henry was stalking me, a line between his eyes as if he were frowning. He really wanted to go out.

I went to the door again and opened it a crack. The snow was worse now, much worse. The line of trees had disappeared, and even the shed seemed far away. I was almost afraid to let Henry out. Before I could shut the door again, though, he darted around me and was gone. I stood there, shivering, trying to see where he was, and then he was back, streaking through the door straight across the living room, into the kitchen, and onto Josie's lap.

I set up my drawing things in front of the window, beginning the rough lines that would turn into Josie. Josie was there on the other side of the room, at the table, fiddling with the radio knob until she found a station with Christmas music. The announcer's voice: "A lovely Christmas Eve morning."

I'd hit the date straight on the head.

The songs began, one after another: "Adeste Fidelis," "Silent Night," "Winter Wonderland," and one

I'd never heard before: "Gather 'Round the Christmas Tree."

I leaned over the paper in front of me so Josie wouldn't see what I was doing. I sketched in the space around Beatrice first, the counter, the popcorn machine, and then began to work on the faces. Every few minutes I'd peer out at the snow coming down. Across the river the mountain was blurred, just a dark shadow rising into the pewter sky.

And then I thought about Josie sitting there, my figure in her hand, staring out the window too as she listened to the music, her face tilted, her eyes sad.

Eleventh Picture

On the Mountain

I never really drew any of this. I tried not to think about it. It kept coming up inside my head, though, picture after picture of what happened that last day. Saturday. Izzy and the Old Man off on some antique hunt all the way up to Masonville. Steven begging me to go fishing. "We'll take the boat all the way down to the rapids," he said. "Bring our lunch."

"You go," I said, barely looking up from my drawing.

"Gonna spend this whole day with a bunch of pencils in your mouth? Fooling around with bits of paper?"

I grinned at him over my shoulder.

Go, Steven, I thought. Get out of here.

And then he went with a great clatter, pail and oars, pole and lures, a sandwich dripping tomatoes

out the side. "You'll probably be sorry in two minutes," he said.

He sounded sorry. "Do you mind?" I asked.

He grinned. "Not really. But I'll be gone all
day, I warn you."

He climbed into the rowboat and I watched
him, his back bent, leaning over the oars, until he
was gone.

I put everything away carefully, my pad and
pencils, cleaned up the tomato mess in the kitchen,
put away the box of Mallomars, shut the refrigerator door, and all the time I was thinking, Three
hours up, three hours back, a cinch.

I grabbed a sweater just in case—it was getting
cold now—and at the last minute I changed my
mind and took a few pieces of paper folded in my
pocket, a few pencils: green, gray, brown, and
black, and the French Blue one. Who knew what I
could use it for, but it was my favorite.

And then I began to climb. It was hot work; I
draped the sweater over a tree limb. After a while I
could feel the pull in my ankles, the rub of my
sneakers against my heels. I stopped at the
halfway point to look down at the house, the snake
of the river, and I could see Steven, a tiny figure
in the rowboat.

I pulled out some paper, made a quick sketch,

and climbed some more. Mud. The Old Man was right: It was deceptive. I couldn't tell it was there until I stepped into it, once covering the whole of my sneaker. I pulled the shoe out and wiped it off with a few leaves.

I was out of breath by the time I almost reached the top, and hungry. Why hadn't I made my own tomato sandwich? There was water, though, a tiny thread of it trickling down from one of the rocks, and I leaned my face into it and drank, and put my wrists under it, and then took the last few steps and I was there.

It opened out, a wide piece of rock, and I danced out onto it, catching my breath. I'd brought dark pencils, but this was a light world. I could see toy houses, and the river, and even the town of Hancock in the distance. There was a tiny silver lake and a road with miniature cars. "It's Christmas!" I shouted.

I said all the things I wanted to. "I'm new," I said. "I'm different."

And in my head I told myself I'd never be mean again, I'd be friendly, I'd go to school and walk up to people. "A new leaf," I said.

I was twirling, dizzy, hungry, and the bubbles inside twirled with me, until I took one step too close to the edge in that muddy sneaker, and then I *was rolling, feeling the sharp edge of a branch tearing into my arm and a stone gashing into my forehead, and finally I was stopped by a huge boulder a few feet down. The wind had been knocked out of me. I lay gasping.*

I pulled myself back up. Not so bad, not so terrible, I told myself, wiping the blood out of my eye, except that I knew I'd never be able to walk all the way down by myself.

I didn't begin to call Steven until much later, until the sun had crossed toward the west and I knew it was late afternoon, and I didn't want Izzy and the Old Man to know I had done such a stupid thing. And even as I called, I knew Steven couldn't hear me.

But he came, of course he came. Just before sunset I heard him, or rather I heard the pickup truck, gears grinding and then stopping, the door slamming, and then he was standing over me.

"I knew it," he said.

"How?"

He narrowed his eyes. "Break any bones?"

"Certainly not."

"I wasted my whole afternoon," he said. "Felt sorry that you were all alone, came back, and—"

"Wasted—"

"Right. I figured it out, though. You weren't anywhere."

"So why'd you bring the truck?" I asked.

"Think I had three hours before dark to walk all the way up here to get you?" He shook his head. "I thought you'd been killed."

"Just wounded," I said, laughing.

We sat on the edge of the rock, watching the sun go down.

Steven pointed. "Our winter place is somewhere over there. You'll see it soon." To the east far below was the summer house, the holly bushes a blur of green, the golden field, the thread of river. It took my breath away.

"I want to show you something," I told Steven. I reached into my pocket for the crumpled-up W picture I had taken out of my backpack before I'd left. "I've had it since I was six."

We sat on a ledge, our feet dangling, and he smoothed the picture on his knee, stared at it, then looked over at me.

"We had to find pictures with W words," I said.

"It's a wishing picture," he said slowly, "for a family."

I could feel my lips trembling. Oh, Mrs. Evans, I thought, why didn't you see that?

"It's too bad you didn't come when you were six." He smiled. "I knew you had to stay with us when you let me win that checkers game."

His hair was falling over his forehead and his glasses were crooked, almost hiding his eyes. I thought of the X-picture day and walking out of school. I thought of sitting in the park on a swing, my foot digging into the dirt underneath.

"I run away sometimes," I said. "I don't go to school."

He kicked his foot gently against the ledge, his socks down over his sneakers.

"Someone called me incorrigible."

Now that I'd begun, I didn't know how to stop. "Kids never wanted to play with me. I was mean. . . ."

Steven pulled his glasses off and set them down on the ledge next to him. He rubbed the deep red mark in the bridge of his nose.

I stopped, looking out as far as I could, miles of looking out. For a moment I was sorry I'd told him. But he turned and I could see his eyes clearly, and I wondered if he might be blinking back tears. I wasn't sure, though. He reached out and took my hand. "You ran in the right direction this time, didn't you?"

And that was it. He knew all about me, and he didn't mind.

"We have to go down now," he said, "before they come back and find out."

I nodded. I stood up, and I could feel the pain shoot through my ankle. I limped to the pickup truck. "I'm glad you came," I said. "I could never have walked all the way down."

"It was a dumb thing to do," he said, "coming up here. Pop would have a fit."

And so we went down. Steven was a sure and careful driver, but it was so steep, and the truck kept going, kept sliding, even with the brake pressed down as hard as he could manage. He pressed and pressed, but the truck gained speed, and just before the end when we would have been all right, when we would have been fine, the truck tipped, and I could see we were going to go over.

And Steven yelled at me. "Jump, Holly!"

The Time with Josie

*L*ate that afternoon the snow tapered off and stopped. I took a last look at the picture, pleased with it: Beatrice, listening to something Josie is saying, both of them with bags of popcorn in their hands. I sneaked it into my room so that Josie wouldn't see it.

I put on all the clothes I could find, and Izzy's boots, and went outside to sink into the soft snow almost to my knees. The cold was shocking. It stung the inside of my nose and numbed my cheeks.

Everything was still. The birds must have found nesting places for the night, and the deer were hiding somewhere deep in the woods. The last slim line of river had frozen; if I hadn't known it was there, I'd have walked right across to the other side. I wondered if the ice would carry my weight yet.

I realized I wouldn't be able to pick evergreen or holly branches from the ground. Anything the wind had brought down was under the snow. I'd have to saw off what I could.

Josie and Henry were framed in the window, waving to me. I reached down to scoop up a handful of white and tossed it at them. Then I trudged over to the shed for the Old Man's saw and found Steven's sweater hanging on the knob, encrusted with snow. I didn't even remember leaving it there. I folded it, put it on one of the shelves, reached for the saw, and spent the last bit of daylight hacking away at branches, making sure not to spoil the shapes of the trees.

The wind wasn't as strong under the shelter of those trees, and it reminded me of something the Old Man had told me. Hunters who were lost would pull the tree branches together with rope, bending them to form a shelter. I loved the thought of that, the trees forming a cozy nest. And then I shivered, thinking of being alone.

You have Josie, Steven might have said.

I love Josie, I said back.

From inside, music spilled from the radio. "All I want for Christmas . . ."

What I want. What I want.

Josie was turning on the lamps now; the house was like a Christmas card with the light shining on the snow. I stood there watching, wondering how far the light might be seen.

I reached up for the last branch, snow spraying my face. No one could see the light anyway, I told myself; it faced the river, away from the road, and no one would be on the Old Man's mountain toward evening after a storm like this.

"You're a snowman," Josie said as I trudged onto the porch, staggering under the bulky branches.

I pulled off Izzy's waders and rubbed my feet until the feeling came back. Josie danced around me. "I have something for your dinner," she said, delighted with herself. "I was saving it for a surprise."

She led me into the kitchen and opened the cabinet over the refrigerator. I thought I knew where every-thing was, but in back of Izzy's old bowls and mixers was a row of treasures: a box of dried milk . . . *milk!* . . . pancake mix, and a jar of applesauce.

"Yes," Josie said with satisfaction. "We'll have apple pancakes for dinner with cold milk."

My mouth watered. A Christmas Eve dinner.

I'll pay you back, Izzy, every cent, if it takes me the rest of my life.

So Josie cooked for the first time, talking to me over her shoulder about Beatrice. "Ornaments sparkle on the tree, and Beatrice lights the candles."

Every time Josie talked about Beatrice she seemed to come alive, I thought; Beatrice and her house. I knew she was homesick. "We'll have Christmas here too," I told her. "I'll set everything up after we eat."

But after I'd finished the pancakes covered with dollops of sweet applesauce, my eyes drooped; I was warm and sleepy. "Let's do it all in the morning," I said.

"Presents," Josie said, a secret smile lighting her face.

I curled up in bed, looking out the window at a pale moon and trees thick with snow, thinking I'd never seen anything so beautiful. I could see movement at the edge of the trees and sat up to see what it was. And then suddenly, a fox, silvery gray with his tail streaming out in back of him, darted across that open space, crossed the ice, and was gone.

I saw a fox, Steven. I've never seen a fox before.

I lay back, trying to figure out what Josie might have for me. Maybe she'd found another package of food. I fell asleep wondering what it was, what I'd like it to be: something sweet, something chocolate, or salty. Potato chips.

Next morning, the sun was blinding. And the shed

glittered like the witch's house in Hansel and Gretel. I lay there, something on the edge of my mind. What was it? Something about the shed? Or was I wondering what the Old Man would think if he knew I was spending Christmas in his house?

I didn't want to think about that. But there was something else. Was it Josie's present for me? An egg was what I really wanted this morning. What I could do with an egg! I'd bake a cake or cookies. I'd whip it up for an eggnog. I'd fry it like a little sun in a pan.

I threw on my clothes. The house still smelled of the pancakes from last night. I went into the kitchen.

At that moment the back door opened and Josie came in, her scarf pulled over her forehead, her nose red.

I wanted to tell her she shouldn't be out there, that it was too cold, the snow too deep. But I'd sound like the stucco woman. I turned back to the stove. "Cocoa with milk," I said.

We hurried through breakfast, and afterward I went out on the porch to shake the snow off the branches before I brought them inside. I covered the mantelpiece, the sharp pine smelling like Christmas, as Josie unwrapped the box of ornaments. "Here's my old Santa Claus." I could hear the tears in her voice as she hung him in the center. "And this one." She held up a thick pink plastic globe. "Ugly, isn't it? It's the only kind we could get during the Second World War."

She went on, telling me the history of each one, until the mantel was finished and the center of the table held a bowl of holly. "We'll even hang a few of those glittery ornaments over the window to catch the light," I said aloud, and to myself, *Please be happy, Josie.*

"Presents now?" Josie asked.

"Maybe," I said absently. I had caught movement outside as I hung the last clear prism.

We watched as seven or eight deer wandered in front of the house, making their way toward the evergreens. Suddenly something disturbed them. Heads back, noses up, they stood stock-still for an instant, then scattered, two to bound across the river ice as the fox had last night, the others in the opposite direction, toward the bridge.

I tried to see what had bothered them. I looked toward the evergreens myself, looked back as far as I could. There was no light anywhere, nothing to make me think about a fisherman being out there somewhere.

I had a quick thought of the night on the mountain with the flashlights like glowworms above me.

It was then I remembered: Steven's sweater, a flash of green in the snow as I backed away from the fisherman that day. I hadn't left it on the doorknob in the shed. I opened my mouth to ask Josie if she had picked it up when she'd been outside. But Josie would never remember. Maybe I didn't want to know the answer anyway, thinking of the fisherman finding us and what might happen then.

Twelfth Picture

A Mountain of Trouble

I couldn't get warm, even though I wore a robe and Izzy's sweater on top of that. Every time I drifted off to sleep that August night, I'd start, thinking someone was there. I'd look around the dark room, but it was empty. I'd close my eyes again, and then I'd think I was falling, my head jerking, arms up, legs braced, a scream in my throat, and that feeling in my chest as we went over the side.

But I really didn't sleep. I kept going over it: the sound first, a screeching metal, tearing, as if the truck were dying, the wheel swerving, a tree slowing us down, its branches cracking, breaking, leaves covering the windshield, a rock ripping at the underside, the truck bouncing now, not so muddy, gravel and roots and Steven's hands off the wheel, the sound of glass shattering, a tire spinning . . .

And then everything was still.

We were almost all the way down the Old Man's mountain, and next to me Steven with his head on the wheel. I reached for him, my heart pounding, shook his shoulder. "Don't do this, Steven," I said. "Don't be dead."

I pushed him back, his head against the seat now, his face white in the dusky inside of the truck. Not a mark on him that I could see, but he was hurt, I was sure, really hurt. He wasn't dead, though. There was a thin pulsing on the side of his neck, his eyes moving under the broken glasses. I took them off gently and heard him say something. Loon Sister, maybe. I could hear the sound of the S. Maybe it was Sorry.

"Steven, I have to get help." I watched him for another moment, then scrambled out of the truck, feeling the pull of my ankle, telling myself I had to do it, had to go as quickly as I could. I began the climb back up, wondering how long it would take to get down the mountain road, cross the bridge, and reach the house. And then I thought, No telephone.

What then?

I was almost there when I saw the sweep of headlights going across the bridge. Izzy and the Old Man coming home?

When they saw me, Izzy leaned out the window, calling, "I bought dishes, Hollis. You're going to love them." And then she stopped. "Child, you're bleeding."

"The truck!" I said.

"What has he done?" the Old Man said. "What has he done now? You can hardly walk!"

It seemed to take forever before lights flickered on the mountain and cars began to park diagonally down below. Turret lights turned and glowed, and an ambulance came all the way from Walton, its siren screaming. They brought Steven down at last, but all I could see was one foot, the sneaker, the socks falling over his ankles.

A policeman shook his head, talking to Izzy and the Old Man as I stood to one side, out of everyone's way. "If it wasn't your mountain, if it wasn't private property, your boy would be in trouble. As it is—"

"As it is," Izzy's voice cut in, "we have to hope he'll be all right."

And I had looked over my shoulder at the Old Man's face, his clenched jaw.

In the emergency room a doctor took five stitches to close my forehead and wrapped an Ace bandage around my ankle. Steven was somewhere inside too, and I didn't even know what was happening to him.

We went home later that night, much later, Izzy and I, Izzy to stay just long enough to put me to bed, to cover me and tell me it would be all right, to touch my cheek and my chin. "Just sleep, Hollis," she said. "Everything will seem better in the morning." And then she went back to the hospital to wait.

I thought about the stucco woman. She wouldn't have been surprised at the trouble I had caused. She would have seen it coming. Would Steven have driven the truck to the top of the mountain if I hadn't been there? And the arguing between Steven and the Old Man—what had Izzy said? "Worse this summer."

I'd messed up the whole family.

Before it was light I packed my things in the backpack. They didn't all fit, so I left a small pile of odds and ends, and the bathing suit that was drying on the line. I tore off a sheet of paper from my drawing pad and wrote the note: It was my fault, all of it. I wanted to see the mountain. I'm going back to Long Island. Please don't come after me. I don't want to be a family after all.

I looked back as I left, to take a picture of it all in my mind, thinking how strange it was to use my running money to run back to the stucco lady. It was even stranger that she let me walk in there so easily, clucking over my bandage, taking me to the doctor a week later to have the stitches out.

Emmy, agency hotshot, came to see me to tell me Steven was going to be all right. "His ribs are broken," she said, "and the bones in his arms are fractured." While her mouth was still open, ready to say something else, I told her "I never want to go back, I never want to see any of them again."

She tried to find out why, but when I just kept looking out the window, banging my feet on the chair rung, she sighed and let me stay with the stucco woman.

I didn't do that, either. I lasted there through most of September, and then I ran.

The Time with Josie

CHAPTER 14

"My cousin Beatrice would love this," Josie said, looking around the room. "If only . . ."

I'd never seen anything so beautiful, so Christmasy either. Pine branches were everywhere. We'd found candles, maybe a dozen, and lighted all of them. The ornaments sparkled in the light.

And then I thought of what Josie had begun to say. "If only what?" I asked.

She shrugged a little. "Beatrice and I spent every Christmas together. She remembers things for me when I forget, things about when we were young." Her forehead wrinkled. "Fishing off the jetties."

I felt a lump in my throat. "She'll be home some-day," I said, but I wondered when that would be.

"Next year?" Josie said.

I looked out the window. I didn't like to think about next year. Where would we be then?

"Just a minute," I told her. "Close your eyes."

I went down the hall for the picture I'd drawn and laid it on the table to flicker in the candlelight. "Josie herself," I said, "with Beatrice."

She drew in her breath, leaning over it, running one finger along the edge. "We're young." She smiled up at me. "And look at that popcorn ma-chine." Head tilted, she spotted Henry batting a piece of popcorn across the floor. "You have to keep look-ing to see everything," she said.

She stood up then and pattered away from me into the kitchen. She came back with a round tin in her hand. "This is from Santa Claus."

I touched the tin. "Where did you find this?"

Izzy's hard candies: Izzy standing on the porch one sunny afternoon, holding a tin out to me. *Lemon drops, and orange. They'll make you sweet, make you lov-ing.* She had leaned forward to touch my shoulder.

"You always have a lump in one cheek," Steven told me days later as I worked my way through the candy. *"It's going to freeze like that."*

Oh, Izzy. Oh, Steven.

I opened the tin and held it out to Josie. "You get first pick." Another thing I had to pay back. I couldn't just take Izzy's candies.

"Take them," I suddenly remembered Izzy saying with a sweep of her arm. *"Take anything, Hollis. I've always wanted a daughter."*

"I have a real present for you," Josie said around the candy in her mouth.

I looked after her, wondering, as she went into Izzy and the Old Man's bedroom and came back with something in her arms. "She's finished at last."

It was my tree figure, with her sea-grass hair cascading down her back, almost half the size of Josie. She looked older than I was, but as I touched her face, the small nose, the large eyes, the tiny scar on the forehead, the arms out, I could see it was me.

But not really me.

I looked closer, studying those eyes that were so sad it hurt to look at them, ran my fingers over those outstretched arms.

"Giving arms," Josie said, nodding, bone thin, like one of the little birds that perched on the evergreen trees. I reached out to her, feeling those small shoulders, and hugged her to me. Tears burned my eyes. "She's beautiful," I said.

"Do you think she looks like you?"

I held her out. "She's not as tough," I said, trying for a smile. "She doesn't look like a mountain of trouble."

Josie shook her head. "Maybe you're tough when you need to be tough. But trouble? What would I ever have done without you?"

Josie put her hand under my chin and tilted it so that I had to look at her. "I wish you could see yourself the way I see you."

"But I'm not—" I began, but she broke in.

"Not good? Not kind? Not there when you're needed? Not anxious to be loved? You know that's not so."

I did cry then, but just for a moment. If I had let myself go I would have had a hard time stopping. And then I saw that Josie was crying too.

"I know you want to go home," I said, a jumble of thoughts in my mind. I wanted to say that we could be a family here, but she wanted to be in her own house, wanted to make Christmas cookies with Beatrice and spend Tuesdays and Thursdays at the movies making popcorn.

We sat on the couch, Henry on Josie's lap, watching the candles glow in the late-afternoon light. The fire in the fireplace sent warm shadows over the wood floor and the walls, and next to me Josie was closing her eyes. Her head went back to rest against the couch, and she was asleep.

I sat there too, half dozing, remembering that Steven's birthday was the next day. It hurt to think about it. I stood up slowly, quietly, and went into his room. I picked up the blurry picture from his dresser, half of the photo dark, the rest all blues and greens, with the faint figure in the center. It was the river, of course; I saw it then, with the holly bushes on the bank and just the faintest view of the Old Man's mountain reaching up in back. There was the row-boat, and I was in it.

How could I not have seen that the other day?

"Hey, stop rowing," he said. *"I'm going to take your picture."*

I looked up at him, feeling the sun on my face, feeling the happiness down to my toes, as he stood at the river's edge and snapped the picture.

"You've got a smiley face," he said. *"We could put you on a stamp and sell it all over Branches."*

"Too bad you didn't take your thumb off the lens," I told him.

"Too bad you dropped the oar," he said. *"It's floating away."*

I put the picture back carefully, then went down-stairs for sweaters and pulled my jacket off the hook.

Something fell out as I did. It was the shell I had picked up the first time I had seen Josie's ocean. I held it up to my face before I put it back into my pocket.

I needed to be outside. I needed to be cold, so cold I couldn't think of anything but the ice and the snow.

Anyting, that's what the stucco woman would say.

Thirteenth Picture

The Conference Room

For all I know this picture might still be in the agency conference room. It's a drawing of a small office with beige paneling on the walls. The paneling is fake wood. There's a table in the center, someone's initials, TR, gouged out of the wood. The picture isn't finished, but Emmy and the mustard woman didn't know that. They thought the girl sitting at the table was me. Of course it wasn't me. This girl was laughing. She was just make-believe.

I wasn't laughing when I sat there. I was sitting as straight as I could, but I could feel my knees shaking.

"Mr. Regan wants to talk to you," Emmy said.

I shook my head, never looking at her, sketching on the paper.

She leaned forward. "He's come all the way down here, Holly."

"Hollis."

"Just see what he has to say."

I shook my head again, but Emmy patted my hand and was out the door.

And then he was there, standing in front of me, and I still didn't look up. "I'm sorry," I said in a voice so low I wasn't sure he heard me.

"It was Steven's fault," he said.

"No," I said.

"He took the truck—" I could see him wave his hand. "Hollis, it doesn't matter. We just want you home."

I thought about standing up. I felt like putting my arms around him, then going out to the car with him. I thought of what it would be like to drive up to their front door.

"I didn't tell Izzy and Steven I was coming," he said. "If I had, they would have come too. I had to make sure you wanted to be with us first."

Izzy would be standing at the door, and Steven next to her. We'd be hugging each other, all of us. There'd be pancakes and hard candy.

But that was just for a moment.

"It wasn't Steven's fault," I said. "I went up the mountain first."

"It doesn't make any difference."

He was blaming Steven. If I went home with

him they'd always blame Steven. "He thinks you're perfect," Steven had said. Before I could change my mind, I shook my head. "I think I'll stay down here."

He tried to talk me out of it. I wasn't even hearing what he said. I stopped drawing; my hands were clenched under the table, and I never once looked up at him. After a while he left.

Emmy came back in with tears in her eyes.

"You want tough?" I asked. "I'll show you tough."

The Time with Josie

CHAPTER 15

*O*utside it was almost dark. A sliver of moon curved over the Old Man's mountain, and a single star was just visible. *"A planet, Hollis,"* Steven might say. *"Get your astronomy in order."*

If I cried again, the tears would freeze fast to my cheeks.

The snow was so dry I could hear the creaking of my footsteps as I went past the holly bushes. No one could guess they were there, mounded up like soft white pillows, and the river in front of me had disappeared.

I stood still to look at it all. I wondered how I could draw that to show the world underneath: sharp, shiny leaves hidden in the snow, the river running fast and cold under the ice.

In my mind was a picture of Beatrice brushing her hair off her forehead. *"Drawing is a language, "* she had said. *"You have to learn to speak it. "*

In the distance was the faint sound of a saw: Someone must be cutting wood for a fire. I closed my eyes. Steven and the Old Man turning their heads. *Roger's saw,* they'd say. *He must be in the apple orchard, or Hopper's finally gotten to that dead elm.*

No, it wasn't a saw. It was the sound of a snowmobile, probably on the other side of the mountain.

A clump of snow fell off the roof of the house. I looked back at it, at the house where I wanted to belong. Huge icicles hung from the eaves, and suddenly I was so cold I couldn't stay outside anymore. Upstairs in my bedroom I sat at the edge of the bed shivering, waiting until I was warm; then I went to my backpack and pulled out my pictures to spread across the bumpy white bedspread.

I saw how much blue I had used in those summer drawings: blue for the river, blue for the Old Man's rugs, blue for Izzy's locket; and green: a smudge of tree, a leaf, the edge of the mountain. Both colors I loved.

The pictures I had drawn of Josie lay in the middle of the bed. Josie on the pier, reaching for sea grass; Josie outside in her tree garden, shades of peach and lilac; Josie happy, Josie where she belonged.

Josie didn't belong here. She belonged in her house

with Beatrice, and Henry, and the irritable pelican on her wall.

She belonged near the ocean.

I sat there for a long time, my head against the headboard, knowing what I had to do. I rubbed my hands, still icy cold. It was four miles to the telephone outside the grocery store, a long walk, but I could do it. I'd call Beatrice . . . ask her, beg her.

We'd go home, Josie and I, Josie to Beatrice, me to another place. I looked at a half-finished picture of Izzy at the cemetery with a vase of daisies in her hand. What had she said that day? *"I wanted children for every corner of the house."* And what else? There was something more she had said, something about Steven and the Old Man. *"It's worse this summer."*

I'd have to stop thinking about Izzy, put all of them out of my mind. Before I left I'd get rid of all the pictures of them, burn the drawings in the fireplace. I'd forget about Izzy and the Old Man, forget about Steven.

I stared down at the drawing of Izzy backing out of the door with my WELCOME TO THE FAMILY cake and saw something I hadn't remembered: the Old Man's hand on Steven's shoulder.

Me, catching my first fish. Steven in front of me with the net, the Old Man smiling. But he is looking at Steven, not at me. Looking and smiling.

And another: Steven hanging into the engine of a

car, just the back of him visible, with mismatched socks, and the Old Man with his hands on his hips, but his eyes are soft.

Beatrice was in my head again. What had she said to me one time? *"Sometimes we learn from our own drawings; things are there that we thought we didn't know."*

My lips were suddenly dry.

I stood up, walked around to the other side of the bed. There they were in the boat. Steven laughing at something the Old Man had said.

How had I drawn all that and not seen it?

Of course the Old Man loved Steven. He was going to love him whether I was there or not. Had I given them up for nothing, the whole family?

What do you know about a family? Steven said in my mind. *You've never had one.*

I remembered what Izzy had said then: *"They have to find their own way."*

I picked up another picture: me with candy in my mouth. Then there was something else floating just on the edge of my mind. Something to do with the radio? Why the radio?

Wait, I told myself. What had Josie said about wanting Santa to bring a radio?

And then I had it. The two of us joking. *"Santa on a sleigh,"* I had said.

"That was a hundred years ago. Now he comes on a . . ."

. . . a snowmobile? To bring the candy? Steven? The pancakes, and the applesauce?

I slid off the bed, the picture drifting out of my hand, my knuckles up to my mouth.

The sweater hanging on the shed doorknob.

Holly on the back step. *"Peace, Hollis."*

I felt as if I could hardly breathe.

And then I was flying down the stairs, my feet barely touching the steps, skittering on the Old Man's shiny floor, coming to a stop in front of Josie asleep on the couch.

I sat down next to her, one hand on Henry's rough fur. "Wake up, Josie," I said. "I want to ask you about Santa Claus."

The Time with Josie

CHAPTER 16

Josie slept through my questions, her head nestled on the couch cushions, and Henry with her, purring faintly with his eyes closed. She slept as I shook her, slept as I begged her, "Please, Josie, I can't wait to know," slept as I offered her soup from a can, Izzy's candy, a cup of tea.

Then at last I gave up. I looked at the black square that was the window. The moon had disappeared behind the Old Man's mountain, and the star was gone.

I went into the kitchen to make something to eat: the rest of the tuna with canned pineapple thrown on top, and a few frosted flakes for crunch. I ate it at the kitchen counter, wolfing it down, made hot chocolate, and when it had cooled a little, put it under Josie's nose. "Smells good, doesn't it? Just open your eyes, take a sip, and talk to me."

She smiled in her sleep as I kissed her forehead, and then I went upstairs to bed, lying awake for a long time, feeling the tick of my heart in my throat.

Maybe the holly had just blown onto the back step. Maybe Josie had found the candy in the house. Maybe. Maybe.

But then as I fell asleep, I could almost hear his voice in my head. *Merry Christmas, Hollis Woods.*

I was awake at the first light the next morning. It was a beautiful day, with sunshine melting the ice on the window. I went downstairs and Josie was still asleep on the couch, but Henry was awake, stretching his skinny legs. I let him out and stood in the doorway, hugging myself, squinting at that glittering world, listening for the sawing sound of a snowmobile.

And then Josie opened her eyes.

I began slowly. "Christmas was yesterday," I said.

She smiled at me.

"Santa Claus is coming . . . ," I sang.

". . . to town," she finished.

"He came to us," I said.

"In all this snow," she said.

"But what did he look like?"

She ran her hand over her face, thinking. "He looked cold," she said.

"And he gave you the candy."

"One time," she said, "when Beatrice and I were little, he brought mittens. Red for Beatrice, blue for me. We each swapped one. All winter, we wore one blue and one red."

I went over to her and touched her hair. "I'm going to call Beatrice," I said.

"Are we going home?" she asked.

"Maybe," I said. "I think so. Can you wait here? It's a long walk to the phone. I'll be gone most of the morning."

I heard a few fragments of song as she wandered into the kitchen. "If it takes forever, I will wait . . ."

I made breakfast for both of us, a heap of frosted flakes; then I layered on sweaters, three pairs of Steven's socks, my jacket, and turned to Josie for one last try. "Where did you get the candy?" I asked.

"It's in a tin box," she said. "Orange and lemon. Makes your mouth wiggle."

"I'll be back." I opened the door, hearing the drip of melting icicles from the roof, and stepped back as Henry darted inside.

Outside I thought at first of taking the road. What difference would it make if I were caught?

But it would make a difference. I wanted to call Beatrice first. I wanted to hear that she'd come to live with Josie.

And suppose she doesn't? Steven asked.

I shook my head. *She will. I think she will.*

I brushed him away, trudging along through the trees, listening to the call of the crows, the screech of the blue jays. And all the time I was listening for that buzzing sound of the snowmobile, telling myself I had made the whole thing up, telling myself it wasn't Steven.

And what if it was Steven? I asked myself. What would I say to him?

It must have been almost twenty minutes later when I heard the faint sound of the motor. It could have been anyone, but still I ran toward the road, trying to pick up my feet in that deep snow.

I saw him, a helmet on his head, thick gloves on his hands, bent over the handles of the snowmobile, and I stepped out onto the road just in time for him to see me and glide to a stop.

I stood there, biting my lip, feeling that river of tears coming at last, waiting for that brief second as he pushed up the visor. "Hollis Woods," he said. "Where are you going?"

"Steven Regan," I said, my mouth trembling. "Happy birthday."

And then we were laughing, both of us, laughing instead of crying.

"Thank you for the candy," I said at last, looking at

his face, thinner, bonier. Something about his eyes seemed older.

"Horrible stuff, that candy," he said.

"And the holly branch."

He tilted his head a little. "Hollis Woods," he said again.

"How did you know I was here?"

He raised one shoulder. "There was a letter from the agency looking for you."

I nodded, thinking about the mustard woman sending lost girl letters to every house I'd ever been in.

"I told Pop." Steven swiped at his glasses. " 'Hollis loves that house,' I said. But did he listen? Of course not."

I swallowed. "You and the Old Man are still arguing."

" 'If she loved that house so much she'd be with us right now,' Pop said. But I knew. I've been here every day except during the big storm."

I was shivering in the cold, the wind blowing around us, my feet beginning to feel numb.

"We've been hoping you'd come home all these months," he said. "Why not, Holly?"

And then I was crying, big sloppy tears. I leaned against the handlebars, making terrible sounds in my throat, and I just couldn't seem to stop.

Steven stood there, his hands dangling in those

huge gloves, and then he reached out, put his arms around me, pulling me toward him.

"The Old Man went down to Long Island when he heard you were missing," he said. "He's going crazy looking for you. He keeps going back and forth."

"Why didn't you tell him?"

"I wanted to do that for you, at least that. Give you time." He paused. "You're famous. Your picture's in the newspapers. A pretty awful-looking picture, if you ask me."

As he rattled on, I kept sniffling and wiping my eyes, and then I'd start to cry again.

"I knew you'd be safe." He took one arm off my shoulder to wave it around. "As long as I kept an eye on you and your friend."

"You have a nerve," I said.

"You'd have starved to death without the food I brought." He frowned and began again. "I still don't know why . . ."

"I thought . . . ," I began, and bit my lip. I'd never tell him what I had thought about the Old Man not loving him. "You were always arguing, and I thought it had to do with . . ." I waved my hands.

"With you?" he said. "Oh, Holly. It doesn't have to do with anyone. I told you that. It's just the way we are."

I stared down the road, not a car in sight, the trees heavy with snow, bent and leaning.

"I'm a slob and he's neat. I forget, he remembers. We drive each other crazy. But it's all right."

I ran my hands over my cheeks, tried to dry them. As simple as that, just the way they were.

"I told you," he said, his head tilted, his eyes smiling. "You don't know about families yet." He leaned back against the snowmobile. "He knew the accident was my fault."

I sighed. "It was my fault."

"Everything has to be your fault all the time?"

I shrugged a little.

"After the accident, Pop said they'd told him you never stayed in one place very long. But he said we were different, and that it must be something else. And that's what it was? You thought—"

"I messed up the family."

"Wait till he hears this," Steven said. "Just wait."

I watched the snow drifting off the trees. *Old Man, I love you.* Steven rubbed my shoulders; he must have seen that I was shivering. "I put the fishing pole away for you in the shed, and looped the sweater over the knob."

"The fishing pole?" My hand went to my mouth. "I forgot about the fishing pole. All this time."

"Ha, Hollis Woods, there's hope for you, I told you

that. I'm going to spend next summer fixing up the old truck. What do you say? Want to help? Want to come home?"

I didn't say anything. I didn't have to. I climbed up on the back of the snowmobile. "Take me to the telephone booth down at the grocery," I said.

He gunned the motor and the snow spewed out behind us as we flew up the highway to call Beatrice.

The Time with Josie

CHAPTER 17

*S*teven stood next to me in that freezing phone booth, his eyeglasses steamy and small puffs of smoke coming out of his mouth. He talked the whole time. "I told Izzy not to worry, that you'd be home by Christmas." He waggled his eyebrows. "Of course I knew where you were."

"Wait," I said, dialing the number I'd memorized all those weeks ago. "I can't hear."

"And the day after Christmas is pretty close." He grinned at me.

Then Beatrice's sweet voice was in my ear, soft and a little breathless.

"It's me," I said. "Hollis Woods."

For a moment she didn't answer. When she began to speak, it seemed as if she couldn't stop. "I've been calling for days, Hollis," she said. "Where are you? Is Josie all right? Do you know where Josie is? Please know. I've been so worried." She paused, really out of breath now.

I closed my eyes: Beatrice worried, Josie unhappy, the Old Man looking for me. What had I done?

"She's with me," I said.

Steven's voice was still in my head even though he was standing right next to me. *If you hadn't made that mess, you might never have come home.*

"Josie wants to come home. She remembers home, but she forgets so much else," I told Beatrice. "The agency isn't going to let her stay there alone. And they want me to go somewhere else."

"I'm coming home, Hollis. I'm coming home right now. Don't worry. I'll move right in with Josie." Her voice sounded excited. "I'm already sick of painting the desert. I need some snow in my life. I need to see Josie and Henry."

Steven clapped his hands together for warmth. "By the way, we started on your room anyway," he said. "I told the Old Man we'd paint it green, green for holly."

"Beatrice, she'll be so glad to see you," I said, looking at Steven, listening to them both at once.

"But the Old Man wanted your room blue," Steven said. " 'Hollis loves blue,' he kept telling us. What does he know? French Blue, he calls it."

I grinned. The Old Man knew a lot. But maybe I wouldn't tell Steven that either.

I talked for another minute, telling Beatrice we'd go home soon, telling her we were all right, we were fine, and then I hung up the phone.

Steven yanked off his gloves with his teeth, reached for more change, and laid it out on the shelf. "I bet you don't even know our phone number," he said as he began to dial.

I could hear Izzy's larger-than-life voice. "Is that you, Steven?"

He handed the phone to me, then let himself out of the phone booth to stand outside, stamping his feet.

"It's me, Izzy," I said. "Do you think I could come home?"

Fourteenth Picture

Christina

The Old Man framed this picture and hung it over the bed in my French Blue room in our winter house in Hancock. The mirror on the opposite wall reflects the picture so it's the first thing I see when I open my eyes in the morning . . . that and my tree figure from Josie.

The tree figure wears the crystal beads Izzy gave me. "They're too small for you now, Hollis," Izzy said as she looped them carefully over the sea-grass head. "They're from my sixth birthday. But I always wanted my oldest daughter to have them."

I tried to match the picture to the W one in my backpack, but I couldn't do it exactly. First, there's a flag in the background of this one because it's Memorial Day, the day we open the house in Branches for the summer each year. It's early in the morning and we're standing on the porch steps with the sun sending beams of light across the river in front of us.

But there are five of us in the picture instead of four. The Old Man, looking a little grim: He's just discovered that Steven left his bedroom window open so the snow drifted in all winter, ruining the wall and buckling parts of the wood floor.

Steven tries to look serious, but you can see the laughter in his eyes. "Holly will paint it up," he said, needling the Old Man. "She'll paint it green. That's her favorite color."

They still argue, sometimes so loudly I put my hands over my ears. When they see me they smile. "It's all her fault," Steven says, and the Old Man leans over to pat my shoulder.

In the picture, Izzy stands in the center, a little taller than the Old Man. She's wearing a loose shirt in that blue I love. "Are you happy?" she asked me as I sketched us all later that day. "Be happy, Hollis, because I am. I've never been happier."

I didn't answer. Instead, I drew smiles on both our faces. I'm the fourth one in the picture, by the way, smiling just a bit. I know I'm thinking of Josie, thinking of running here with her a year and a half ago. If I hadn't done that, I wouldn't have this picture, wouldn't have any of it. I'd still be running.

Every month we go to Long Island to see her in her kitchen with Henry, and the pelican, and the tree figures she still carves, while Beatrice patters around fixing tea for all of us.

Josie doesn't remember exactly who I am anymore. She loves me, though, I know that, and always reaches up to touch my cheek. Sometimes I wear her brown hat with the veil, and then I see the recognition in her eyes. "Hollis," she says. "You saved my life." Maybe she doesn't know why, but still she says it, and I always tell her it was the other way around.

And Henry? Ancient, but still feisty. "That cat's as tough as you are," Steven says to me.

Henry looks at me, and it's almost as if he winks before he closes both eyes above a wide yawn. We speak the same language, that cat and I.

I have a new last name now. It's Regan. I love the sound of it. I haven't forgotten Hollis Woods, who wanted and wished, fresh as paint, a mountain of trouble, so I sign my drawings using the three names. They all belong to me. Emmy and the mustard woman both like the idea of that. They show up regularly to say hello, nodding and smiling as if they were the ones who changed my whole life. I don't say anything. I know they're relieved to have me off their hands and settled. And I have to say I can't blame them for that. I have to say, too, that I even smile back at them once in a while.

But the picture, and why it doesn't match the first one, the W picture: It's because I'm holding my sister, Christina, six weeks old, in my arms.

She looks quiet in the picture, contented, sucking on her thumb. But she's not always like that. And when she cries, we run to her from wherever we are. We stand over her bassinet smiling at her, cooing. And Izzy always puts her arms around me. "You brought us luck," she says.

So there are five of us now: a mother, a father, a brother, and two sisters.

A family.

About the Author

PATRICIA REILLY GIFF is the author of many beloved
books for children, including the Kids of the Polk Street School
books, the Friends and Amigos books, and the Polka Dot
Private Eye books. Her novels for middle-grade readers in-
clude *The Gift of the Pirate Queen; Lily's Crossing,* a Newbery
Honor Book and a *Boston Globe–Horn Book* Honor Book; and
Nory Ryan's Song, an ALA Notable Book, an ALA Best Book
for Young Adults, a *School Library Journal* Best Book of the
Year, and a Society of Children's Book Writers and Illustrators
Golden Kite Honor Book for Fiction. Her most recent Random
House book was *All the Way Home,* published by Delacorte
Press.

Patricia Reilly Giff lives in Weston, Connecticut.